GUNS

*A harvest of stories, essays and poems
from Blackbeard to Billy the Kid and
from Ernest Hemingway to N. Scott Momaday*

SPEAKING VOLUMES
NAPLES, FLORIDA
2016

GUNS

ISBN 978-1-62815-583-9

GUNS

Acknowledgments

Grateful acknowledgment is made to the following for previously published material:

We Just Went On: A Memoir. George Kolb, Irie Books, 2013

Hunting With Hemingway. Hilary Hemingway & Jeff Lindsay, Diversion Books, 2016. Reprinted by permission of authors and publisher.

Two Sons of China. Andrew Lam, Bondfire Books, 2013. Reprinted by permission of author.

The Kebra Nagast: The Lost Bible of Rastafarian Wisdom and Faith from Ethiopia and Jamaica. Edited by Gerald Hausman, St. Martin's Press, 1997. Reprinted by permission of author.

Day & Night: Bolinas Poems. Aram Saroyan, Black Sparrow Press, 1998. Reprinted by permission of author.

TANGLED BYLINES, a father and son cover the twentieth century, The University of Missouri Press, November, 2016. Reprinted by permission of the author.

Cecelia, Dancer, Elisavietta Ritchie, Guy Wires, Poets' Choice Publishing, 2015 Reprinted by permission of the author.

The Woodcutter Talks, "Vagina". Bob Arnold, Longhouse, 2016. Reprinted by permission of the author.

Table of Contents

Epigraphs

The guns are the rulers and mankind merely the trigger finger.
Marcus Garvey

A gun will give you the body, not the bird.
Henry David Thoreau

It feels like men's eyes are guns.
Alice Winston Carney

When a man hits a target, they call him a marksman. When I hit a target, they call it a trick.
Annie Oakley

Let your gun therefore be the constant companion of your walks. Never think of taking a book with you.
Thomas Jefferson

Editor's Introduction

Gerald Hausman

This all began a few years ago when I read "Momaday's Gun" by Kiowa author N. Scott Momaday. I could not forget the story, it stuck in my head. It rubbed against my heart. I asked Scott whom I knew from years before when I published a collection of his stories, in an audio series. His book was titled *Storyteller*. But here was a story about Billy the Kid's pistol that should have been in that collection but was written much later.

I asked Scott if he would consider writing a longer work focusing on the gun, its history, and the legends surrounding it perhaps, and he answered: "Why don't you do it, Gerry."

I replied, "I think you've turned the table around on me."

He laughed and said, "Maybe I have."

That phone conversation stayed with me, and time went by and one day I awoke to my mission. The book began with Billy and the West and a legendary six gun. But it didn't want to end there. It wanted to go on and on.

As Fate, the Muse, the deities or the dark lords of firearms would have it, this book wouldn't write itself, nor would I write it myself. It would be written by many others, and so it has; and so we have it now. A collection of surprising familial, historical, philosophical, and literary tales of guns and human culture.

It is my contention that we will never get rid of the gun. It is a part of us as much as the stick, the club, the knife. And it is exactly as Roger Zelazny had his character Hugh Glass say in the novel *Wilderness*—"No race, nation, or tribe had a monopoly on cussedness; it just seemed a part of being human."

When I asked for submissions for this anthology, I did not ask for anything specifically. I said, "If you have a story about guns, send it to me." I did not elucidate, persuade or barter. I wanted writers to find their way into this collection and not be badgered into it. I wanted them not to know, exactly, what it was all about. I wanted them to say something, anything, about guns in their attic and in their holster. And, most importantly, their family history. For there is a spiritual history of firearms as well as a historical one.

D.H. Lawrence once said that Americans could not speak frankly about sex because they did not have the vocabulary to do so. He said this almost a century ago and it is still true today. We lack the actual words to be able to have a non-generic conversation about sex. Not to mention many other things that we carry around in our heads, knowingly or unknowingly.

It is the same thing with guns. We don't really know how to talk about them except in the political sense—and this usually comes out in a fiery bloom of passion harking back to the Second Amendment, which, as we know was about arming militias during the Revolutionary War, not about the personal rights of citizens. It was about preparedness for imminent war.

Perhaps the time has come to find words that express the feelings, the unseeing hatred and blind love bestowed upon our old friend the gun. If it has a barrel and shoots it is in this book.

Gerald Hausman

From A Revolutionary War Diary

Avril Little

March 5, 1770

I feel someone come close and take me forcefully by the hand.

I turn to see who—Peter Wright, my next-door neighbor, my best friend, my almost-brother.

"My father says your family ought to hide out in our stable," he says.

I pull the hood of my coat over my head. My feet are loose in my unlaced boots, and I bend down to tie them. But Peter pulls me up by the arm. "Just keep moving, Avril. Follow the crowd."

There is not much choice. There is a huge mass of people forcing us along towards Griffin's Wharf.

"Why did you come out here?" Peter asks.

"Minor Owens got hurt in the fighting and I heard him crying for help and I thought I could help him."

The crowd pushes us faster and harder.

Where is poor Minor Owens?

My feet are cold and my body is already tired from the elbowing all around me. The night is one great bonging of bells.

At last we're on King Street.

"There's Minor," I say to Peter. "His face is all bloody."

"There's not much we can do about it, Avril, we're pinned."

"Minor!" I cry out.

He sees me, reaches for my hand, but doesn't quite make it. Someone knocks him down, I grab at his shirt, catch it, and it tears, and then we're pulled apart and the crowd surging like a river forces us all the way to the Custom House on King Street.

5

I'm still calling, "Minor! Minor! I'm here!" But he's gone from sight. Peter has been holding me up the whole time, and a few times, my feet were wheeling under me but weren't touching the cobbles.

When Peter and I are almost up against the little sentry box in front of the Custom House, I see Minor again. This time I grab his shirttail, and hold tight to it.

I look into his blood-spattered face. He doesn't seem to know me anymore. Both of us are jammed into the mire of bodies and the little boy is torn from my grasp, and that's the last time I ever see Minor Owens.

Before us a row of redcoated soldiers. They stand almost elbow to elbow, and facing them so many angry Radicals with clubs and other weaponry. Mostly catsticks–those bats used in stickball—lots of broom handles and hatchets and the like.

Right in front of me there's an iron-faced British soldier, someone I know. His name is White and I have seen him often in the British Coffee House. But now here he is in front of the meanest bunch of Radicals.

They taunt him— "Fire away, you bloody lobsterback!"

White: "Do your worst, you Rebel scum."

"They will," Peter says.

There's a volley of ice balls, Peter pulls me into a crouch with him, but one of the ice balls cracks against my arm. I start to cry and then catch hold of myself, and stifle the tears.

Peter says, "Are you all right, Avril?"

"I'm scared more than hurt, but I did feel a hard pellet of ice strike my arm."

He wraps his arms around me so his back's against a fresh storm of rock-packed snowballs.

Then a hail of stone laden iceballs. Some of them crash into the pine-battened walls of the Custom House and chip the wood like musket balls.

The British soldiers are dodging and dancing to keep from being hit. One of them is knocked solid, stumbles, falls, goes down hard. An iceball whistles in and slices him on the skull. His eyes roll back and he lies there as if dead and I watch the blood come snaking down the side of his ashen face.

More and more of these homemade missiles are thrown at the brave band of resolute soldiers. A little stone pings against my chin. I bite my tongue, there's that bittersweet, salty taste of blood filling my mouth. I'm spitting and swallowing.

An old man next to me says, "These British think they can tax us, beat us, jail us do anything they want any time they want." He shouts out –"You can't kill us all, you rotten bloodybacks."

I'm wondering why I ever left the safety of our house. It actually comes to me now that Peter and I could be killed. I feel his strong arms around me, but I don't feel any more safe than anyone else.

Neither Peter nor I can move. Redcoats in front, Radicals in back. We're trapped.

I hear a voice I know well. Henry Knox, the bookseller. He's telling the British Captain to lay down his arms. "Tell your men," he warns, "not to fire. One shot and you're dead!"

Peter says, "I have an idea. Get down low as before, I'm going to drag you a little ways out of this mess."

Before I can say anything, he squats and starts pulling me through the bullying crowd. We make small progress, banging into knees, but mostly people try to make room for us.

In a little while Peter's managed to get us to the east side of King Street, and a ways off from the riot.

"Take your last look, Avril," Peter tells me.

"Why?"

"Because, some of those people will be dead if you look back again."

He pulls me toward Pudding Lane.

A wild man claps Peter on the back.

I recognize him: Sam Gray, Peter's uncle.

"Don't run, lad," Sam says. "You're out of danger now. Where you going in such a hurry anyways?"

"I'm taking Avril home."

"I'm going up front where I can butt them like a goat," Sam says cheerfully, and then he works his way back the way we've come.

For a second or two, we watch him. I see a soldier throw his arms out and go down hard. His musket clatters on the ice, and the Radicals roar.

Then all hell breaks loose at Custom House Commons. The Radicals are pitching their clubs, rock-laden iceballs, anything heavy they can get a hold of including loose cobblestones they've pried up. Redcoat muskets crack back at them. I see little spearheads of flame spitting from their long dark barrels.

The soldiers kneel on the Custom House steps, and one after another, fire on the rioters.

I see Sam Gray again. He's been hit.

Peter runs over to help him. People are scattering—not so brave and teasing as they were before. By the time Peter gets to his uncle, John Hinkling is there to help him. Sam all wobbly, and crazed. Mr. Hinkling lifts Sam up by the shoulders, Peter too, from behind. That's when I see the open hole on the side of Sam's head. I look too long—Sam's brains start spilling on the snow. I feel my knees go out from under me. My head is whirling and the Commons is spinning like a crow in a storm. I hear Peter saying, "Avril, wake up!" But the Commons spins round and round, and the light before my eyes fades and like Sam Gray I am not there anymore.

***

Editor's Note: The diary from which this fragment came describes the early conflict between the colonies and Great Britain. The Boston Massacre has received less historical attention than the battle of Lexington and Concord. It was however a significant uprising if only because of the accidental way it was precipitated. Also because of the seemingly outmatched colonists who used snowballs against British muskets.

BROWN BESS

The True Death of
Edward Teach, Alias Blackbeard

B.A. Botkin

Blackbeard enters fourteen men over the bows of Maynard's sloop, and Maynard's men were twelve.

And so it began.

Blackbeard and Maynard fired the first shots at each other, whereupon the pirate took the first blows, and got shot.

But now Maynard, seeing his advantage, stepped back to cock a second pistol, then came forward and took a swipe from Blackbeard's cutlass.

Now they were even, one and one. However, from behind Blackbeard came skulking one of Maynard's men, dealing the pirate a quick cut on neck and throat, and the blood did flow.

The two men, with a third parrying about, were—shall we say, warmly engaged in battle. There was as said earlier Blackbeard and his fourteen, Maynard and his twelve, all round about and fairly dancing with murder in their eye.

And the sea, blighted by the work of these men, was tinctured red.

And the deck was slippery and salty, to be sure.

The close in-fighting of Blackbeard and Maynard proceeded apace. Maynard fired a shot. Blackbeard took it and stood it well fighting on with great fury, his cutlass gleaming and streaming with blood. Yet in the fray he got five and twenty wounds from all four quarters—five by shot, twenty by cutlass.

And then a cat gull passed over the sunken copper sun and a frigate bird flicked over the waning mangrove moon, the man known as

Blackbeard cocked his pistol for the last time, stared Maynard full in the face and grinning dropped deader than gnat's dust.

So it ended. Or almost, I say.

Those of the scholarly profession say that Blackbeard had thirteen wives, and that is a telling, and largely untold, but unlucky number. But that did not do him in. Moreso his mean disposition; moreso still, his many bloody wounds.

Maynard's men lost no time severing the pirate's head from his well-used body and they hung that head from the yard-arm of their ship. Nor did they wait for the body to draw a single saltwater mosquito. In a trice they tossed the lifeless and headless form into the murky Carolina sea ....

Neither legend nor history can explain the rest.

For, it is said, the deadman swam three times round the ship.

So they say ... or once said more than once, and so it stuck.

But I ask you now—Would a deadman so dispatched, and suddenly liberated from this earthly coil, feel like engaging in a such a silly swim? And this, after losing his men, his ship, his booty and his head all in the same communion of time?

Would he now?

I think not.

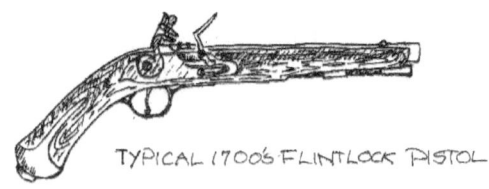

TYPICAL 1700's FLINTLOCK PISTOL

Wild Bill Hickok and
the Great Socorro Bear

J.W. Buel

Bill had two excellent pistols and a Bowie knife when he met the most terrible bear in the West. The cinnamon is well-known to be a worse enemy, when angered, than a grizzly and this was a mother with cubs.

She moved toward the man guided by her maternal instincts.

Bill moved toward the bear guided by his material instincts. Point of fact, he was guarding a group of freight wagons and the bear stood in his and their way.

The bear, instead of showing fear, showed her intention of attacking him.

Curious thing about Wild Bill, he had no fear of anything mortal. Partly because he wasn't certain he himself was mortal. Whatever he was, he thought it was an easy matter to kill a bear. This was a presumption in which he was most seriously mistaken.

Now the bear came within twenty feet of Bill and he drew forth one of his pistols and fired. The ball struck her squarely in the forehead. Fact is, the cinnamon has "brain protection." That is to say, a brain pan so thick that the ball from an ordinary rifle will make no impression on it.

Except to put the beast into more than a normal state of rage.

Bill discovered from the bad result of this first shot, that he had an antagonist bent on a mission that might, as we say, afford more than the usual apprehensions. He was too far from his wagon to get on top of it. And by the time he realized this, the bear was right on top of him.

He then discharged his second pistol, injuring the animal's left fore-leg. But as he dropped his pistol and withdrew his long knife, the bear grappled him.

The struggle which now ensued was the most desperate ever known.

Bill buried the knife rapidly in various parts of the bear's body. He also slashed her throat. But while doing this, the bear tore his shoulder dreadfully, crushed his left arm from the elbow down, furrowed his chest with her six inch claws, and split his left cheek wide open.

There he was in the agonizing embrace of the infuriated Socorro who showed no sign of weakening or slowing down.

They fought on, the two of them, until the ground on which they fought was saturated with bear's blood and man's, and then Wild Bill fell.

The bear came down like a towering tree right on top of him.

Nor did the furious creature stop mauling him. He could hear as well as feel her jaws crunching away on his limp left arm.

That did not prevent him from using his right, good arm to punch his Bowie knife in and out of the bear's belly. This caused her to rise and then trip over her own intestines. She got so entangled in them that she assisted in her own destruction. And fell over dead, tied and gagged in guts.

It was hard to tell who was the worse off—the dead bear or the half-alive man. They were both shredded messes of meat, blood and bits of bone.

Matt Farley and his friend, the two freighters Bill was traveling with, hauled him back to Santa Fe where frontier surgeon Dr Sam Jones spent two months restoring his patient to such a condition that he could at least walk and resume work again. Still and all, the wounds he received that day he bore to the grave. Upon that I will swear.

And anyone who wonders why he was called Wild Bill needs to look at the picture more closely. Some say he got that name by shooting the blarney out of the McCandlas gang. But, listen to me, now ... because I heard it direct from his wife.

"The McCandlas bunch was no more than seven, but that Socorro bear was seven in one."

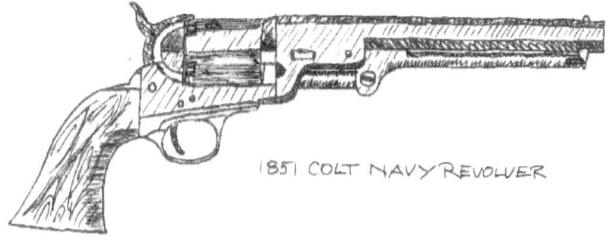

1851 COLT NAVY REVOLVER

The Ballad of Jim Bird Quinney

Bill Worrell

When I was age nineteen or twenty I had a friend who was age 21 purchase a handgun for me. I was under age, so I could not legally buy a pistol. It was a cheap 22 caliber H&R (Harrington & Richardson) six round revolver. It cost about $22.00. This was in 1952 or 1953. When my dad found out what I had done he went ballistic—no pun intended.

Today—and yesterday, too—and tomorrow and the days and daze after that I still have and will have a ringing in my ears given me by the incredibly loud report of that cheap pistol, along with shotguns, rifles, and other handguns I have owned.

I used to enjoy firing all sorts of guns. Today they are locked in safes and I seldom fire one. Neither Ellie nor I enjoy loud explosions.

But back to the 1950s: Daddy was angry and probably quite fearful that I might injure or unintentionally kill someone with that weapon. More than that, he had a story from his youth that exacerbated his fears. It was several years before he told me the tale. Here it is, all true as far as I know, the story—and the ballad I wrote several years ago.

The Ballad of Jim Bird Quinney

Jacob Worrell met William Raleigh Quinney at dental school in Philadelphia. I have Quinney's ticket to class, dated 1847. I have both their sets of dental tools. Quinney, fifteen years Worrell's junior, convinced him to return home with him to Sweetwater, Alabama, and they both practiced dentistry there. Worrell was also a blacksmith and Quinney was also a surveyor. Jacob Worrell married William Raleigh

Quinney's daughter, Lula, and they had three children: Evie, the oldest, William Ingersoll, who changed his middle name to George due to the atheistic implications, and John Mays, who became my father.

W. R. Quinney had five sons, among them John, and James Bird. Practically all the Quinneys migrated to the Maypearl, and Colorado City, Texas areas sooner or later. With James Bird it was much sooner! It was also to different places in the State.

The story has been told and retold, among the Quinneys, the Barkleys, and the Worrells. The setting was near Sweetwater, Alabama. The year was 1902. There was a baseball game somewhere out in the country near Sweetwater, and after the game my father was riding in a buggy driven by his favorite uncle, John Quinney. Enter the Popes, a family who hated the Quinneys about as much as the Quinneys despised them. One of the Pope boys came up behind the buggy and reared his horse, causing its front feet to land in the carriage. This over-turned the vehicle, and the Pope boy galloped off, laughing. Uncle John was furious, and my dad was crying.

"Are you hurt?" he asked.

"I think so," the frightened boy sobbed.

John Quinney uprighted the buggy and quirted the horse to Aimwell, to a small country store. There, on the porch, stood the Pope boy (As I do not know his given name, I refer to him as "Billy.") Uncle John jumped out of the buggy and grabbed Billy by the collar. As his fist was flying the Pope boy stabbed him three times in the heart—with a knife hidden in his sleeve. Uncle John, though mortally wounded, held on, and pulled his own knife, opening the blade with his teeth. He sliced Billy Pope almost in half. As this was happening, Jim Bird Quinney, John's brother, went to his saddle bag and withdrew his revolver. The Pope boy was a goner from Uncle John's cut, but Uncle Jim placed the pistol to his head and blew out his brains.

It was a bad, bad scene, and a horrible event for anyone to witness, especially a ten year old boy. The bodies were covered with a sheet or a blanket on the front porch of the Aimwell, Alabama store. W. R. Quinney was summoned. He pulled back the cover, looked at his dead son and at the dead Pope boy Lyon beside him and moaned, "So it finally came to this!"

Jim was afraid of both the law and the retaliation of the Popes. He fled the scene and hid out with some friends, named Boozier, until a train ticket could be secured and he could exit Alabama, his home sweet home.

Family legend states that he donned woman's apparel when he would go to the out house to avert suspicion of the Popes and the law, and that a part of his exit was made in house of darkness, by horse-back. What we do not know is how much fear was kindling in the hearts and minds of the Pope clan, for there were three formidable Quinney boys left, along with kith and kin. Even in late 1800 photographs there is a look in the Quinney boys' eyes that makes one wish not to tangle with any of them.

Jim Bird Quinney went to a town almost in the center of Texas, named Coleman. There he dropped his surname and met a woman who came to know him only as Jim Bird. They were married in Sweetwater, Texas, some seventy miles to the northwest. My father told me, about 1968, that they lived briefly in Shallowwater, a few miles west of Lubbock, and then went to Wellington, in the Texas Panhandle. There, James Bird lived and died, and only after his death was it revealed to his wife and children that their husband's and father's real name was Quinney, not Bird, and he was from Sweetwater, Alabama. I was told that this caused resentment by Jim Bird Quinney's descendants.

Uncle Jim Bird Quinney's daughter, Lurlene, died this week in Tucson (at the time of this writing), and this brought to surface this family tale and my old notion to place a proper gravestone upon the site of his burial.

John Mays Worrell died April 4, 1977, and his passing was a catalyst for uncovering more family history. It was at that time that I penned *The Ballad of Jim Bird Quinney*, or some half-baked version of it. It is somewhere in my old journals. Remembering what I could of the chorus or the bridges, I re-wrote it yesterday around noon, and this morning about 4:00 a. m.

***

One can see what hateful hearts and unbridled passions not subdued can do. These were young men in their primes. They killed each other 96 years ago (again, at the time of this writing). The tragedy is that they are still dead. They will be dead for a long time, and they will never get to view life through calm, mature eyes.

> In Maringo County
> In the year of 1902
> The Pope Boys and the Quinneys
> Had themselves a hot blood feud.

Verse I

> Nobody understood
> Just hard those boys could hate
> Always tracking down each other
> Forever tempting fate

> Billy Pope was hunting trouble
> Always looking for a fight
> Always out to get the Quinneys

The Ballad of Jim Bird Quinney

Even though it risked his life

So two young men would die
By the gun and by the knife
And another live in hiding
For the rest of the his life

My dad was only ten
When he saw his uncle die
Stabbed by Billy Pope
Right before his tender eyes

Uncle John pulled out his knife
And the Pope boy he did slice
Through stabbed through his own heart
And knowing he would die

Jim Bird witnessed this event
To his saddle bag he went
He returned
With his trusty forty four

He put the gun to Billy's head
And he blew that young man dead
There were two hot headed boys
In the cold blood on the floor

A Pope had killed a Quinney
A Quinney killed a Pope in turn
A fatal case of passion

From an evil fire that burned

Verse V

It was an eye for an eye fight
Trade a brain for a heart
Forcing Jim to leave his town
And make a brand new start

Oh! Folks come to Texas
For many a reason
Bridge I And mostly they deal with the law
Sometimes bad horses
Sometimes bad women
But they learn to be quick on the draw

If you're going to Texas
And you plan to stay healthy
Keep ahead of the Popes and the law
Bridge II Shake with your left hand
And keep your piece loaded
And learn to be quick on the draw

If you're going to Texas
And you aim to stay healthy
Bridge III There some things you better learn
(Talk here) Never ask a man what his last name is
Don't ask him where he's from
Don't ask him where all he's been
Or what he might a done

Resume And keep ahead of the Popes and the law

The Ballad of Jim Bird Quinney

Singing
> Shake with your left hand
> Keep your gun loaded
> And learn to be quick on the draw
> Hey Jim Bird Quinney
> You took up for your kin
> Though it cost you your home
> You could never go back again

Verse VI
> After ninety bitter years
> To your lonely grave I came
> With a tombstone and an epitaph
> That bears your real last name
>
> It's been ninety-seven years
> And still nobody knows
> What stirred up all that trouble
> 'Tween the Quinneys and the Popes

Verse VII
> Some deep, dark, hidden secret
> Only known to them and God
> Buried with their sorrows
> Beneath the Alabama sod
>
> Yeah buried with their sorrows
> Beneath the Alabama sod.
>
> In Maringo County

Reprise
> In the year of 1902
> The Popes and the Quinneys
> Had themselves a hot blood feud

The new grave stone reads:

HERE LIES A NOVEL
MY UNCLE
JAMES BIRD QUINNEY
KNOWN TO HIS FRIENDS AND FAMILY
AS
JIM BIRD

Billy and the Gun

Frances Bonney Jenner

"Advise persons never to engage in killing."
William Bonney, Billy the Kid

Just before dawn when the full moon silvers the dark sky, I awaken into the dreamtime. The time when heaven and earth join and everything is possible, when memory and consciousness are one and there is no past, only present.

I listen.

I hear Billy's mother, Catherine, and she sings. It's a lullaby and Billy is newly born. Catherine rocks Billy in her arms, she swings and sways him, holding him tender as dandelion down drifting and joyful as the smile of a light heart. She sings to Billy in a voice that's pure and there's an Irish lilt to it. Billy snuggles in close to his mother's heart and a bond that shapes both hearts begins.

It never ends.

***

When Billy is about four years old his father dies, leaving a tiny puncture in Billy's heart. Catherine dies an early death as well, she dies from tuberculosis, then called consumption, and Billy, at fourteen, is left without a mother or father. At that moment of Catherine's death, that tiny pinprick rips itself into a big hole, right in Billy's heart, dead center. And Billy carries that hole and the burden of it, carries it for the rest of his 21 years.

I have always felt a kinship with Billy the Kid. As a young girl grow-ing up in Texas, I was born into a Bonney clan, and like Billy, I carry the name Bonney. My family and I traveled together to Roswell and Lincoln, New Mexico, Billy the Kid country, when I was a young teen. I remember my father and I both being intensely interested in Billy's story. He and I climbed the steps of the Lincoln County courthouse where Billy was held prisoner until he escaped and we saw the bullet hole still in the wall where Billy shot his guard, Deputy James W. Bell. My father hoped I would one day write about Billy, and in hoping he passed along a badge of honor to me. I take the badge but as I write I think, how dare I, when the great writers already have, Scott Momaday, Michael Ondaatje, Walter Noble Burns and others. But I make a decision. I will write, because I must. My writing will be my own way of telling Billy's story. And as I write, I move into a deeper kinship with Billy.

Most everyone knows of Billy the Kid and he fascinates us still, even in our modern day. The authenticated photo of Billy playing croquet discovered in 2015 is worth $5 million, and his original photo, $2.5 million. We all want a piece of him, even though he lived such a short life, 135 years ago. Billy is a historical celebrity and his charisma, even in death, knows no boundaries.

Lawlessness ruled the culture of the 1870s American west, even in a civilized town like Silver City, where Billy lived during his early teen years. Men placed a high value on gunmanship, wearing six shooters as commonly as a shirt, hat or trousers. David Abraham, a successful town merchant there and father of Billy's friend, Louis, killed three men with his shotgun, supposedly in self-defense. The town downplayed and excused the killings by a respectable citizen, did not even bring Abraham to trial and they justified the killings as necessary. And that was Billy's norm in Billy's time and place.

To understand how the gun intersected with Billy's life, I read intricately researched histories of Billy by Frederick Nolan, Michael Wallis, and Miguel Otero, Jr. and others, as well as oral histories told by those who knew Billy during his time. Stories about Billy abound and I read and ponder them, some accounts true and others pure myth, and with the help of historians, I try to honor Billy by being aware of the fabrications so that I can hold true to his story, if possible. And as I get to know Billy through story, I begin to see the connections between the way Billy lived his life and he way he wielded his gun.

According to his Silver City friend, Harry Whitehill, Billy stole his first six-shooter from his stepfather Henry Antrim. Billy had endured a difficult history with Antrim. After Billy's mother's death in 1874, Antrim abandoned Billy and his younger brother to be cared for by local Silver City friends and residents. On his own at fifteen and broken by his mother's death, Billy struggled to make a living and carry on without any family support.

At that time Billy befriended George Schaefer, a fellow boarder at Mrs. Brown's local boarding house in Silver City where the two roomed. Harry Whitehill said of George, "This fellow George, he liked to steal." George had stolen clothing from the local Chinese laundry. Realizing that Billy was poor and needed clothes, he influenced Billy to agree to hide the clothes in his room at the boarding house. Mrs. Brown discovered the stolen clothes and turned Billy in to Sheriff Whitehill, Harry's father. Hoping that a jail sentence might reform Billy, Whitehill jailed Billy for being an accomplice. Meanwhile George skipped town.

Perhaps it was Billy's love of reading dime novels that gave him the idea for the jailbreak, that and something about his character that he refused both then and later to be confined to any kind of jail cell. Billy made his first jail break by climbing up the jail's chimney flue and jumping from the rooftop down to a ridge below. He must have been desperate or he wouldn't have sought out his stepdad Henry Antrim, but he did, finding his way to Antrim's mining cabin in southeastern Arizona. Antrim refused to help him, saying to Billy, "If that's the kind of boy you are, get out." Billy retaliated by stealing Antrim's six-shooter and some clothes. And that's how Billy acquired his first gun.

When Billy was seventeen years old, army contractor Sorghum Smith hired Billy to help out at a hay camp near Camp Thomas, in the Bonita area of Arizona. Billy asked Smith for his wages after working at the camp a while. Sorghum gave him $40.00. With the wages, Billy went to the post trader and bought his second gun, a .45 six-shooter, and a belt, holster and cartridges. That Friday night in August, 1877, Billy arrived at George Atkins's cantina. Gus Gildea, a local cowboy who knew Billy said, "He came to town dressed like a 'country jake' with 'store pants' on and shoes instead of boots." There he had an altercation with a local smithy, Windy Cahill.

Windy Cahill knew Billy and had tormented him on many occasions, ragging him, throwing him down, ruffling his hair, slapping and humiliating him in front of men in the saloons in the area. This wasn't the first time that Billy had been bullied. While living in Silver City, Levi Miller, a Silver City blacksmith, and his rough friends often harassed Billy, due to his slight physical build. Miller's wife, Margaret, even said to Levi, "Stop it. You are making him mean." Windy Cahill's repeated bullying along with Billy's previous history in Silver City may have been one of the reasons that Billy bought the gun.

Those who knew Windy Cahill said he was always blustering and blowing hot air. According to witness Gus Gildea, Windy insulted Billy as he was playing poker that Friday night at the cantina, calling him a pimp and Billy fired back verbally, calling Windy a son of a bitch. Billy, slight at five foot eight and 135 pounds was no match physically for the burly, stout Windy. Windy, big as a bear, grabbed Billy, wrestled him down to the floor three times, pinned his arms and knees, and slapped his face. Billy called out, "You're hurting me. Let me up." Windy replied, "I want to hurt you. That's why I got you down."

They continued to wrestle, rolling each other across the floor towards the cantina door and outside near a cattle chute. A crowd of men followed the two out the door, shouting, hollering. While they wrestled, the fight between them riled up those who stood by and watched. Then, Billy managed to pull out his six-shooter and shove it into Windy's stomach. Windy felt the gun jab into his gut, straightened his body slightly, tried to grab it and couldn't. Billy cocked the six-shooter and fired. The sound of the bullet shot pierced the night and silenced the crowd and Windy's body slumped down onto Billy. Billy wriggled free, ran towards the hitching post where John Murphy's racing pony was tied up. Billy grabbed the horse and rode away. (He later returned the horse).

Windy died not long after. Local Justice of the Peace, Miles Wood, convened an inquest, finding Billy guilty of "unjustifiable" murder. Billy became a boy outlaw on the run and at large, however he was never caught or arrested for this murder that might be considered self-defense. Historians believe that Windy was the first man that Billy killed. Billy's brand new six-shooter did the deed and for the first time Billy had solved a problem with a gun.

Billy's friend, Frank Coe, related his memories of Billy in his interview with Miguel Otero, governor of New Mexico from 1897-1907. He said to Otero, "Billy explained to me how he became proficient in the use of firearms. He said that his age and his physique were handicaps in his personal encounters, so he decided to become a good shot with both rifle and six-shooter as a means of protection against bodily harm."

And Billy did become a good shot, not surprising, as he had shown early on that he had a competitive drive. As a young teen, Billy excelled at singing (he was the lead singer in the school talent show). He became an accomplished dancer at the Silver City town *bailes* (dances) and later at Ft. Sumner, and he showed promise at school while living in Silver City. He learned to speak Spanish fluently and became a proficient gambler at Poker and Monte, even before leaving Silver City. "He must have had good stuff in him," said his friend John Meadows, "for he was always an expert at whatever he tried to do."

So it rings true that he also applied himself to learning to be a skilled marksman, especially as the gun increasingly supported his livelihood and assured a means of survival in a culture that honored the gun above all.

Frank Coe said of Billy that he was one of the best shots that he ever saw, in fact, so good that Billy could hit a bear's eye far enough away that you could hardly see the bear. During the time that Billy lived with Frank, he shot Frank's barn full of holes, practicing from every possible angle on and off his horse, using ten times as many cartridges as anyone else. He would ride his horse at a full gallop while shooting snowbirds sitting on the fence, hitting about one bird in three and sometimes one after another.

Lily Klasner wrote in her frontier memoir, *My Life Among Outlaws*, that Billy practiced continually, shooting both handgun and rifle while riding horseback. He was adept at shifting his body to the side of his mount and firing from that position while his horse was on the run, just as the Apaches did.

Deluvina Maxwell, a young Navajo woman and servant for the Maxwell family who befriended Billy in Fort Sumner, knew Billy well for many years. She said, "He could whirl his gun about on his finger and then shoot. A boy from Vegas tried to act like him once and shot and killed himself."

Francisco Gomez, who knew Billy in Lincoln, said of him "He would throw up a can and would twirl his six-gun on his finger and he could hit the can six times before it hit the ground."

Even Pat Garrett, hired on as sheriff to hunt Billy down, said of Billy that he shot well under all circumstances, whether in danger or not. Garrett admitted that Billy was so quick to react with a gun, that if Garrett hadn't killed Billy by surprise that Billy would have escaped.

As Billy acquired gun knowledge and expertise he began to use the gun as an equalizer but also to effectively even any perceived score, as in the case with Windy Cahill, and to act out his own version of the wild west gun code, an eye for an eye. He carried a '73 Winchester rifle, several kinds of pistols, such as a .38 caliber colt revolver called the Lightning, and his favorite .41-caliber Colt double-action Thunderer, that he could fire rapidly without cocking.

Sister Belinda Segale, a Catholic Nun, writes in her memoir, *At the End of The Santa Fe Trail,* of her meeting with Billy in Trinidad, Colorado.

Sister Segale had tended to the bullet wounds of one of Billy's pals, who she called Schneider. One afternoon, Segale went to Schneider's room. She noticed he was uncharacteristically joyful and wondered why. He sat upright, leaning against his propped-up pillow. A smile had replaced his usually dour expression.

"What's got you so chipper this afternoon, Mr. Schneider?" she said.

He reached up, scratched his head, nodded and said, "Well, Billy, he's coming. Yeah, he is, 2 pm next Saturday. And do you know the four physicians who refused to dig the bullet out of my thigh?"

"Yes," she answered, "I know three of them, one is our Convent physician, Dr. Beshore."

Schneider grinned and it was a gleeful grin. "Well, Billy's gonna kill 'em, all four of 'em. That's why he's coming."

Segale felt her body tighten. "It disturbs me that this pleases you. I can't stand by and let that happen," she said.

"Well, what are you gonna do about it?" Schneider replied and gave her a look that said, you ain't powerful enough to stop Billy for righting those doctor's wrongs.

A big fear rose up in her. It got her in a stranglehold although she managed to hide it. She didn't feel brave, but maybe God would show her a way. She put on a brave face and her words came out impulsively, as if God spoke for her, and what she said surprised her.

"I'll meet Billy and his partners, all of them, 2 o'clock next Saturday," she said to Schneider.

"Well, I've been telling Billy all about you and I know he'll be right pleased to meet you," Schneider replied.

Segale had no such feeling, but she kept that and everything else to herself.

At 2 pm the following Saturday, Segale stepped lightly into Schneider's room. Four men gathered about his bedside. Schneider introduced Billy and the others, calling Billy the captain. She thought something about him stood out, like a leader, and he did have those blue eyes everyone talked about, steely and clear with a fixed purpose and they looked right through her. She couldn't tell whether the purpose in them was bad, good, or just plain neutral, but she didn't turn her eyes away from him, and she didn't know exactly why. He looked young, maybe 17, innocent too, not at all what she expected, and she could see why they called him 'Kid.'

He wore a sombrero, but removed it as a sign of respect, and nodded to his partners to remove theirs, too, and they did. Then he welcomed her saying, "We are all glad to see you Sister, and I want to say, it would give me pleasure, to be able to do you any favor."

She didn't expect him to be gentlemanly. She could hardly register in her mind that this was Billy, the notorious outlaw. He didn't seem like one, and this unexpected way of his didn't make sense.

She had preplanned and practiced her next exact words, to make sure she would not back down from them, and she replied to him "Yes, there is a favor you can grant me."

And without asking about the details of the favor, he reached his hand out toward her, smiled, and said, "The favor's granted."

God must have moved her to take Billy's hand and she did. His hand was small, like her own, tough but gentle, warm, and chiseled perfectly to trigger a gun, but it felt right, somehow, holding his hand in hers, even though it shouldn't have, but she relaxed anyway, thinking God's ways are mysterious and that she must find the courage to ask him for what she wanted, in spite of her conviction that Billy would go back on his word.

And she did ask, saying, "I understand you have come to scalp our Trinidad physicians, which act I ask you to cancel."

Billy seemed genuinely surprised. He looked over at Schneider and the look that passed between them must have had some meaning that she did not understand.

Billy, still holding her hand, looked back at her, and said, "I granted the favor before I knew what it was, and it stands."

Deep inside, she sighed with relief and felt a great joy, but contained it so that the men would not know. She could hardly believe what she heard.

Billy continued then, saying, "Not only that sister, but at any time my pals and I can serve you, you will find us ready."

She felt humbled and thanked him, giving his hand a squeeze. It was a genuine gesture that she made before releasing hers from his and leaving the room. She thought then that Billy had both devil and angel in him and wondered if somehow God had had a hand in what had just happened.

Apparently, Billy's code went both ways.

On the run because of Windy Cahill's murder, Billy made his way to Lincoln County, New Mexico in October, 1877. Within a year, Billy became involved in the range war, an armed struggle for financial control of Lincoln County between the corrupt Murphy-Dolan ring and the Tunstall-McSween ring. The Murphy-Dolan ring controlled local government, business, and law enforcement, and the Tunstall-McSween ring was attempting to break the power of Murphy and Dolan.

Billy went to work for John Tunstall, a wealthy English investor and business partner of Alexander McSween, a Scottish lawyer, and both relative newcomers to Lincoln County. Tunstall became Billy's boss, friend, and father figure, some even say. Frank Collison, a Texas cowpuncher who knew Billy, said, "I heard him (Billy) say that Tunstall was the only man who ever treated him as if he were freeborn and white."

In February, 1878, Tunstall and his cowboys, including Billy, rode his six horses and two mules to Lincoln. The Murphy-Dolan gang had secured a court order to take the horses, but there was a dispute between the two groups as to which horses were to be handed over. Tunstall had hired his cowboys to protect him. Unaware of any coming danger, they had spontaneously scattered in search of wild turkeys when members of the Murphy-Dolan posse came upon Tunstall and found him temporarily alone. Murphy and Dolan had persuaded Lincoln's Sheriff William Brady to appoint the posse to take Tunstall's horses. When the posse came upon Tunstall, they surprised him and then murdered him in cold blood. Tunstall's body was recovered and brought in the next day and laid to rest in the parlor of McSween's home. Billy is purported to have paid his respects, taken off his sombrero, looked up at Tunstall lying dead on a table, and said that he would get some of the murderers before he died. And that was the beginning of the Lincoln County Wars.

The code was on and in force.

Billy became part of the Regulators gang of gunmen, whose mission it became to hunt down the ring members who had murdered Tunstall. Numerous gun battles between both sides followed that took the lives of both rings.

The final battle of the Lincoln County War took place inside and around Alexander McSween's adobe home that faced the main street in Lincoln. The Murphy-Dolan gang had trapped fourteen of McSween's Regulators and McSween himself in the McSween home during the five-day siege. The Murphy-Dolan gang of forty men stationed themselves across the street. Colonel Nathan Dudley from Fort Stanton had brought cavalrymen, infantrymen, and a howitzer canon to Lincoln as a support for the Murphy-Dolan gang.

On the last day of the battle, the Murphy-Dolan men set fire to the McSween home, forcing those inside to take a stand and eventually make a run for it. The house burned slowly, room by room, until only one remaining room, the kitchen, stood. Those inside hoped to escape in the dark of the night, if the house would last that long, and it did. By evening, the home's ceiling began to fall in, smoke filled the one room, and the walls threatened to collapse. McSween had no experience as a fighter and he grew more and more helpless in the situation.

Billy took charge, saying, "Mack, now we must run for it, it's the only chance for our lives."

Billy and four other Regulators acted quickly. They broke out of the house in the dark of the night with the burning house illuminating their charge out and in doing so they drew attention and gunfire to them from the Murphy-Dolan side so that McSween and others remaining could follow, protected by the cover of their gunfire.

The first five men, including Billy, armed themselves with guns and rifles, Billy carrying a six-shooter in each hand. A barrage of gunfire came at them as they ran out of the house. Billy shot continuously into the night using both six-shooters as he raced towards the safety of the Bonito River. He and three other Regulators managed to reach the river and evade the gunfire.

Only Harvey Morris, a law student, was gunned down. McSween and the second group hesitated rather than taking advantage of the cover Billy and the others had given them as they escaped and as they broke out, McSween and three others were killed, but five others made it out alive, one of whom was Genie Salazar.

Walter Noble Burns interviewed Salazar after the Lincoln County War and he published some of that interview in his book, *The Saga of Billy the Kid,* published in 1925. In the interview, Salazar said, "Billy the Kid was the bravest man I ever knew.... A little while before we made a dash for our lives, the Kid rolled a cigarette. I watched him. It seemed just then as if he had about a minute and a half to live. But when he poured the tobacco from his pouch into the cigarette paper he did not spill a flake. His hand was as steady as steel. A blazing chunk of roof fell on the table beside him, barely missing his head.

'Much obliged', he said; and he bent over and lighted his cigarette from the flame. Then he looked at me and grinned as if he thought that was a good joke."

Pat Garrett is known to have said of Billy that his skill as a gunman in combination with his nerve is what made him such a dangerous and effective gunman. And others who fought alongside Billy expressed the same sentiment about his iron nerve, especially when in a battle situation.

In December, 1880, Pat Garrett, sheriff of Lincoln County at that time, hunted Billy and four of his gang, following them to Stinking

Springs near Fort Sumner where they hid out in an old stone forage station. Garrett and his posse trapped the gang there and forced them to surrender. Billy was jailed, brought to trial and convicted for the murder of Sheriff William Brady during the Lincoln County War, and sentenced to hang. All of the surviving members of the war on both sides had been indicted for the many killings that took place. However, Billy remained the only survivor who was actually tried, convicted, and sentenced.

Billy said to a Las Vegas reporter after his capture at Stinking Springs, "At least two hundred men have been killed in Lincoln County ... but I did not kill all of them." And after his trial and conviction in Mesilla in April, 1881, Billy was quoted in the *Mesilla News* as saying, "Think it hard that I should be the only one to suffer the extreme penalty of the law."

After the sentencing, Pat Garrett and his deputies transported Billy to Lincoln County where they jailed him in the county court house, previously used to house the Murphy-Dolan store. Garrett and his deputy guards Bob Olinger and James W Bell shackled and handcuffed Billy and put him northwest corner of second floor of the courthouse where he could see out a window onto the street below.

But after a week of being jailed, Billy somehow procured a gun, or managed to get Bell's gun, and killed Bell while still shackled and hand-cuffed. Billy then grabbed Olinger's Whitneyville ten-gauge shotgun propped up inside and hobbled over to his jail room window. He cocked the shotgun and waited for Olinger to return from having dinner across the street at the Wortley Hotel. When Olinger heard gunshots he came running back to the courthouse. That's when Billy shot and killed him from the open window, ironically using Olinger's own shotgun and riddling him with thirty-six buckshot fired at a range of less than ten feet. Billy then crashed the gun barrel over the windowsill and threw the broken shotgun down onto Olinger's body, saying "You won't corral me with that again."

Billy and Olinger had a particular hatred for each other and made no secret about it. Olinger had turned abusive while guarding Billy, taunting him by poking him with his shotgun and telling him to make a run for it, so could blow him to bits. Olinger had also killed John Jones, Billy's friend, treacherously, by shooting him in the back.

After shooting Olinger, Billy found two six-shooters and a Winchester from Garrett's gun supply and with them he made his way out to the courthouse second floor balcony where, according to the *Santa Fe Daily New Mexican* newspaper written a few days later on May 3, he told the Lincoln townspeople gathered outside that he didn't want to kill Bell or anybody but when Bell tried to run, he had to kill him and would kill anybody who tried to stop him.

As I consider these stories about Billy and make meaning of them, I wonder if they show us what the gun meant to Billy or if we can ever possibly know? Did Billy use his gun skill, bravery and nerve to simply support his big need for revenge? Or to fill up the holes in his heart riddled by abandonment and betrayal? Was he a cold-blooded killer, as myth would have it? Maybe there's more to it, I think. Perhaps Billy also used the gun to right perceived wrongs (and he was certainly applauded for this by the local Lincoln Mexican-Americans victimized by the Murphy-Dolan gang). And maybe it was about Billy staying true to his own personal code of ethics and living life on his own terms. Possibly this is what Billy meant when he said to a Las Vegas reporter after his capture at Stinking Springs, "I wasn't the leader of any gang, I was for Billy all of the time."

And surely Billy felt justified in using the gun to escape from the Lincoln County courthouse jail, aware that he had been unjustly convicted and held for the murder of Sheriff Brady in the Lincoln

County War. Brady had been shot down by several of the Regulators and no real proof that Billy killed him ever surfaced. The Murphy-Dolan ring had rigged Billy's murder trial. They wanted him out of the way and they held the power in the courts. Governor Lew Wallace, too, had promised Billy amnesty, but he reneged on his promise.

But when it finally came down to it, it seems plausible that Billy's central purpose for using the gun had more to do with his own protection and survival than anything else, as he told Frank Coe. Billy was willing and able to use the gun no matter what and at any cost, hence the murder of Bell to protect his own skin, making certain the likelihood of Billy's own premature death.

Billy's passion for survival in a wild and murderous environment made the gun an ideal companion for him. By the time Billy escaped from the Lincoln County jail, he and his gun had become inseparable, and given the circumstances of Billy's life, that was understandable. It wasn't just that Billy always carried his gun, like many others of that time, which he most evidently did. I imagine that it was as if his gun was a part of his own body, like an extra arm or leg. And when the law took his guns away by force, he soon found a way to get another one or two or three. Perhaps Billy thrust all of his hurt and lust for survival onto his guns, so much so that his identity actually merged with the gun and he and his guns were no longer separate objects, if such a thing can happen.

Many wonder how many Billy killed with his Colt six-shooter and Winchester rifle.

Billy often said the number was 21, one for each year of his life. And maybe he knew. However, he is only credited with killing four, Windy Cahill, Joe Grant, and Bob Olinger and James W. Bell.

During my last visit to Lincoln in 2014, I asked the Courthouse Museum docent that question, "How many did Billy kill?" She replied automatically and without thinking, probably because she had been asked that question a million times, and she was protective of Billy, saying, "Well, he only killed 4 men, and 3 of them, Cahill, Grant and Olinger, well, they were bad men."

Eventually Billy's accumulated deeds led to his death at age twenty-one by a bullet from Pat Garrett's Frontier Colt six-shooter, which had belonged to Billy Wilson, one of Billy's friends and a fellow Regulator, captured by Garrett along with Billy at Stinking Springs.

After Billy's break from the Lincoln jail, Garrett and his two deputies, John Poe and Kip McKinney took action to track and hunt Billy down, spurred on by Governor Lew Wallace, who offered a $500 reward for Billy's capture. Garrett suspected that Billy may have been hiding out in Fort Sumner. Garrett, Poe and McKinney arrived there late evening, July 14th, 1881, and immediately made their way to Pete Maxwell's home to question Maxwell about Billy. Poe and McKinney stood waiting on the porch just outside Maxwell's bedroom while Garrett went inside to awaken Maxwell.

Billy knew the Maxwell family well, including Pete, and he had been hiding out in Fort Sumner. At the moment Garrett entered Maxwell's bedroom, Billy happened to make his way there, too, unaware of Garrett's presence.

Poe said that Billy carried a six-shooter, a .41-caliber Colt Thunderer, in his right hand when Pat Garrett broke the cowboy code of a fair fight, surprising and shooting Billy in the dark of Pete Maxwell's bedroom. Billy also held a butcher knife in his left hand for cutting a slab of beef intended for his dinner. Poe's account makes it clear that Billy died the way he lived—struck dead by a bullet that pierced his left breast above his heart. Stopped in the midst of life, age 21, by the weapon that he had lived by.

And Billy probably preferred a gun killing to hanging. Billy's friend John Meadows said that Billy somehow got a piece of strychnine, folded it up in a paper, and stuck it inside his boot when jailed in Lincoln County. He planned to poison himself rather than hang.

***

The dreamtime comes to me whenever I am writing about Billy. Sometimes I hear his mother just before sleep. I hear her singing.

> *"Oh, Billy, oh Billy, oh Billy, oh.*
> *No Billy, no Billy, no Billy, no.*
> *Don't, Billy, don't, oh*
> *Oh Billy, Oh Billy,*
> *I love you so."*

Catherine's song, sung in the brogue of Ireland in a soft alto, clear and cool, frosty as a fresh November morning. Her voice comes through the mists of time and consciousness, through light and nature, through space and resistance.

Choice of Weapons

Jane Lindskold

"I don't think Mr. Yammer went because he wanted to." The alley was too dark for Prudence to see the shop girl's expression, but she could smell the anxiety that rolled off of her in waves. "Don't go looking for him. It'll only get you into trouble."

A narrow band of yellow lantern light showed as the young woman eased open the door that would let her back into the shop. "Might not do *him* any good either."

The flickering yellow-white band widened only enough to admit the woman's slender form. Then it closed, leaving the alley in what, for most, would be the near absolute darkness of a moonless night. Prudence wasn't bothered by the darkness, not nearly as much as she had been by the young woman's words, and what they implied about the fate of someone she liked and respected.

When Prudence had arrived in town two days ago, her business had included visiting a local gunsmith who'd done work for her in the past. That the man wasn't there, that someone else was now selling dry goods from what had been the man's workshop, home, and store, these weren't the problem. The problem was how Prudence's sense of smell gave lie to the words offered when she asked where she could find Yammer.

"Yammer? Don't know what happened. Just noticed one day his shop was shut."

"Ol' Yammer? He moved on a couple months back. He'd been sayin' he wanted to go back to his folks."

"Yammer? No idea. Shut up shop one day. Left work undone, too. Folks had stuff returned to them, though. He didn't steal nothing."

Moving on wasn't uncommon. Prudence herself was what most folks would call a drifter, no fixed address, not owning much beyond her two horses and what gear they could carry. That people didn't bother her much had something to do with the tools people like Ol' Yammer crafted, the six-guns and rifle, both of which she handled like the expert that she was. The other reason Prudence didn't get bothered more was the vague, undefined rumor that drifted with her, the rumor that people who treated Prudence Bledsloe poorly had a tendency to have bad things happen to them.

As a beneficiary of rumor, Prudence knew its scent, subtle and misdirective, knew it as well as she knew the scents of fear, of apprehension, even of indignation. All these blending together were a heady perfume, one that made her more, not less, curious regarding just what had happened to the gunsmith.

The shop girl's words had given Prudence her first solid clue. Up until then, Prudence had figured that someone had forced Yammer out of business. Nothing the girl had said had given lie to this, but that bit about Prudence getting into trouble if she kept sniffing around… If Ol' Yammer had just been forced out of business, then the problem should be over. This implied it was not.

Prudence went about her business, keeping her mouth shut, but her ears, eyes, and, most importantly, nose, open. Yammer hadn't just made repairs. He made his own pieces from scratch, as well as customizing store-bought guns. For this, he'd used a small forge, as well as a suite of materials with very distinctive scents.

If the shop girl's reaction was anything to go on, then whoever had made away with Ol' Yammer was local. The girl wouldn't be worried otherwise. But Prudence found not a whiff of the gunsmith. Using her need to have her own rifle and handguns overhauled as an excuse, Prudence gave a closer inspection to the two gunsmiths in town, but again found no indication that Yammer was there, working in secret. Buck and Trick, her two horses, needed to be re-shod, so she took them over to the blacksmith. There again, she drew a blank.

Prudence hadn't expected to find Yammer in town, but she'd wanted to eliminate the possibility before casting further afield, especially since that casting would be much more dangerous. She'd also wanted to be around town long enough to go from new face to just another drifter, here today, forgotten tomorrow. That wasn't hard. Between the stage lines and the port, people came and went so frequently that anyone who was in town more than a couple of weeks was practically an old-timer.

She settled into rooms at a boarding house run by a highly respectable widow. Next she took clerical work at a local shipping company hungry enough for folks who were both literate and possessed of a head for figures that they didn't worry about references—or how much iron they were packing in the folds of their skirts.

She'd applied for work at the shipping company because just about everyone who came into town had business there. While she was no beauty—not with her pale yellow-brown eyes and undistinguished brown hair—she dressed nicely and lent a note of class to the place, or so the bosses said when they gave her a place in the large front room.

Seated demurely at her desk, Prudence copied invoices, made out tickets for stage and ship, and, by encouraging chatter from the sailors, soldiers, and cowhands who came through, started learning about the communities surrounding the town. These were largely ranches and farms, semi-independent, except when it came to transforming their product into cash and cash into raw materials.

Led by her nose for rumor, Prudence narrowed the likely places down to three. The first was a large farm and vineyard, perpetually hungry for labor and not particularly happy when laborers decided they could do better elsewhere. The second was a ranch that specialized in fattening up cattle—some of which might not have been acquired with the permission of their original owners. The third was a longer shot—a boarding house and tavern with an unsavory reputation for turning a blind eye to press gangs.

If Yammer had been pressed, there was little Prudence could do for him. Anyhow, although pressing was the easiest way to make someone vanish—short of killing him—that didn't fit the shop girl's warning. Prudence had long learned that most hunts were done between the ears of the hunter. You learned game trails, watering holes, likely grazing spots. Finding a missing person—or rather a person who'd been made go missing—wasn't much different. Although she disliked the farming operation on principle, they didn't seem the sort to either want or need a highly skilled gunsmith.

By contrast, the Oliver Ranch fit the profile nicely. It had been founded by one Bartholomew "Bar" Oliver, who had a ruthless appetite for profit, but otherwise was considered a good enough neighbor. In time, he passed his holdings onto this three sons: Bart, Chuck, and Jack. Under their administration, the ranch's brand—a simple O with a bar in the center, a visual pun on Bar Oliver—had come to be known as the "Bar Nothing," because that's what folks said, the three brothers would bar nothing to get their way.

All Bar Nothing cowhands went armed. Sure, guns were tools of the cowhand's trade, no less necessary than ropes and saddles. Even if ranchers didn't have to cope with the sort of folk who had a blurry idea about the line between "mine" and "thine," guns had practical uses as well. They could be used to deal with coyotes, mountain lions, and other four-legged hunters who considered cattle herds as potential larders. They might be needed to execute an injured cow or horse.

But the Bar Nothing hands went more heavily armed than was precisely necessary. Even more interesting was that the ranch's owners had a liking for the finer things in life. That included guns with intricately embossed grips and elaborate ornamental engravings on the metalwork.

Prudence got a good look at those guns because one or the other of the Oliver brothers was in and out of the shipping office every couple of days, either making arrangements for shipping cattle to where they'd be transformed into kegs of pickled or salt beef—items in high demand by both the Navy and private fleets—or checking on something or another they'd ordered, including expensive brandy, spices, and, oddly enough, chocolate and molasses. All three brothers had a sweet tooth.

Even at her first glimpse, Prudence thought the grips on the Oliver brothers' hand guns showed Ol' Yammer's distinctive style, a conclusion that only strengthened with repeated viewings. She'd noticed Yammer used patterns that were subtly different from the usual. These guns seemed to bear his mark—and she was pretty sure that this wasn't just a hold-over from Yammer's having had a local shop. Working guns—and these were working guns, no matter how pretty—got beat up, but these never got *too* beat up, which seemed to argue that someone was available to keep them as good as new.

Patience is the mark of a good hunter, and Prudence wouldn't have lived as long as she had if she wasn't a very good hunter indeed. So, even though she wanted to rush off and check if her guess was right, she waited until she learned that the Bar Nothing had just sold several hundred head of cattle. Hands would be needed to drive them down the coast to their final corral. Then the cowboys would likely be released to blow their pay at a town a bit farther from home.

When Prudence was certain the herd was well away, and Bart and Chuck with it, she finally gave slack rein to patience. She took her dinner early, then casually mentioned to her landlady that she would be going out to visit a friend. The landlady only nodded. Whether or not she'd heard any of the rumors about Prudence, she had made clear she didn't care what her tenant did as long as she gave no trouble and paid her rent on time.

Still, even the highly tolerant widow woman might have raised an eyebrow if she knew what Prudence was about that night. After losing herself in the evening bustle, Prudence vanished into a copse of trees that had hosted both courting couples and lynch mobs in its time. If anyone saw her heading that way, they'd assume she was meeting a beau, but Prudence doubted anyone remarked her movements, for she'd gone out of her way to be unremarkable.

The copse was untenanted. With the ease of long practice, Prudence swiftly divested herself of her attire—most of which, including the cumbersome undergarments required by a lady of good standing, had been left in her room. She rolled up the remaining clothing to minimize creasing and placed it, along with her slippers and stockings, in a small bag. This she tucked into a hollow beneath a gnarled tree root.

Then she hunkered down and—faster even than tellers of tales would say it could be done—changed from a naked woman into a lean, grey-furred she-wolf. Under the necessity of exercising Buck and Trick, Prudence had already scouted the terrain for several miles around the town, taking special note of arroyos that not only carried water in the rainy season, but were year-round highways for four-footed kind. An added bonus was that even natural vegetation tended to be thicker in such places.

Leaving the copse, Prudence dropped down into an arroyo and padded along, completely hidden from human view. She realized she probably didn't need to worry. Although wolves were no longer common along the coast, there were plenty of coyotes, some of which grew to considerable size. Even if someone glimpsed her in the dusky half-light of evening, they'd likely take her for a coyote.

Prudence had been born a werewolf. Despite temptations, she had adhered to the guidelines her long-dead mother had taught her more faithfully than most Christians followed their creed. As long as she did not eat either wolf or human flesh or blood, Prudence would have control over both shapes. However, either giving in to the simpler way of the wolf or cannibalism would rob her of her freedom. One would lock her in wolf-shape altogether. The other, though, that would drive her mad.

The prohibition against consuming human flesh and blood was another reason Prudence had learned to fire a gun at a young age, and kept in daily practice. Relying on her wolf form, although far easier, would ultimately spell doom.

Prudence's nose, sensitive even when she was a human, told her when she was nearing the ranch. She lingered in the arroyo, both for full dark and to accustom herself to the heavy smells of cattle, dogs, assorted livestock, sweat, manure, and the like that went into the odor picture of the place. On her daily rides, she'd come close enough to note the location of the ranch's buildings: main house, cookhouse, bunk-houses, stables, chicken coops, servants' quarters. Latrines were tucked behind a stand of cottonwoods that flourished as a result of the extra fertilizer. Cattle were gathered in pastures some distance from where the humans lived. Kitchen gardens were cultivated in the area between.

At this hour, Prudence's biggest concern was the dogs, but many of those would be gone with the herd. Others would be guarding the cattle that remained. She felt pretty certain that she could face down any dogs who chanced upon her. Even the bravest knew—as their humans did not—that there was something different about her. Unless pressed, they usually chose to back away in combined fear of the wolf and deference to the human.

When full dark fell and human activity dropped as low as it would, Prudence slunk from cover and circled the grounds, seeking to isolate the scents that would lead her to a gunsmith. There were guns here aplenty, so she couldn't rely on just the scents associated with them. In anticipation of this hunt, she'd familiarized herself with odors unique to the gunsmith's craft, as a more usual hunter might study up on how a grizzly differed from a black bear, or a mule deer from a white tail.

Preparation paid off, and before long Prudence caught the scents she sought. She knew they might not lead her to Ol' Yammer. Likely the Bar Nothing had someone who could do routine gun repair, but if didn't prove to be Yammer, she could turn her search elsewhere. But, as Prudence slunk from shrub to shadow, closer and closer, she felt sure she had located her quarry.

Beneath the gun-related smells she now distinguished other scents, half-forgotten until her nose was reminded: ginger and fish, tea and rice, combined in ways she'd only encountered when visiting Ol' Yammer's shop. The scents were accented by a tangy note, like and unlike that of pickles.

All the scents were centered on a cabin that stood a little ways from the other buildings within a small grove of trees. It wasn't large— probably no more than one room. Windows on three sides were open to let air circulate; the door, which faced away from the compound, was also open. The cabin stood flanked by a small garden patch on one side, a pump conveniently near.

Light, probably from a single oil lantern, dimly illuminated the interior. Through the open windows she glimpsed a man moving about. Although he never turned to face the window so she could see his face, his shining dark hair, worn pulled tightly back and wrapped in a sort of bundle, was as she remembered.

Confident now, yet never forgetting caution, Prudence belly-crept closer, letting the shadows hide her. There was something about Ol' Yammer's gait that seemed off. She wanted a closer look. If he was injured, that might complicate any rescue attempt. And was he indeed a prisoner? The door *was* open, yet she found it interesting that outside of this immediate vicinity, she had caught no trace of his scent, not even near the cookhouse or other public areas where it might be expected.

Trusting the darkness to hide her, Prudence dropped back behind the trees, angling so that she could look through the open door without being seen herself. Her night vision was better than that of either wolf or human, and she watched as Ol' Yammer went about what was clearly a before bedtime routine, putting things on shelves, splashing water from a pitcher into a bowl, washing his face and teeth. Nonetheless, it was not until he came out to pour the dirty water into the garden patch that she figured out why he moved so oddly.

Ol' Yammer wasn't injured. Instead he wore ankle shackles, heavy ones, that made him shuffle when he moved. So he *was* a prisoner, and this explained why the open door and slightly isolated location were no invitation to escape. Probably someone came by to check on him periodically. With that heavy, shuffling gait, he'd be easily tracked down before he could get far. Ol' Yammer was being kept as a slave.

Doubtless, the owners of the Bar Nothing had some facile explanation they had given to their hands, but they might not have needed much.

Thing was, even these days, with folks saying that the War Between the States had been fought as much to end slavery as to keep the Union intact, people were still too comfortable with the idea of slavery. The Spanish who'd first settled this part of the West had regularly taken Indians as slaves. Heck, some of the Indians had kept slaves, being not nearly so particular as to what race those people were. And lots of the whites who had drifted West after the war had been from the slaveholding states, looking to make a new life for themselves. Prudence had seen plenty of evidence that, for some of those, that new life often involved trying to keep alive some of the traditions of the old.

So, whether you called a person a slave, or an indentured servant, or even just someone paying off a debt, there were plenty of excuses for making people work for you, whether or not the person doing the work agreed to the terms of hire.

Ol' Yammer was just the sort of person to fall prey to someone who took a fancy to having a private gunsmith. He looked to be an Indian of some sort, with shining black hair worn long, almond eyes so dark brown that they were nearly black, and skin that, while not the reddish-brown that got Indians popularly called "Redskins," was a golden brown that certainly wasn't any of the shades from pink to tanned brown commonly called "white."

Prudence didn't know what tribe Ol' Yammer came from. Didn't think she'd ever heard him mention it, but that didn't matter. Whatever Yammer's tribe, he wasn't living with it, so probably no one who cared knew he was missing.

Or rather, she thought, *those who do care are too scared to act.*

She considered what to do next. She'd been careful not to leave tracks, especially in infrequently used areas, but it was too much to hope she could manage repeated visits to the ranch without leaving a trace. There were plenty of dark hours left, so maybe she'd better use some of them to talk to Yammer, find out if he was even interested in escape, before she put her mind to making plans.

Prudence waited until Yammer had snuffed his lantern and had a chance to settle down. He'd left the door open—maybe even had instructions to do just that unless the weather was nasty. When she was sure all was still, she made a fleeting dash from the trees right in through the open door, shifting from wolf to woman as she ran.

It wasn't easy, but she'd had a lot of practice with such things. In fact, the intermediate human/wolf form could be right useful at times. Once she was on her own, Prudence had practiced until she could slip between forms without hesitation. Really, the only inconvenience was her lack of clothing. She wasn't particularly body-conscious, but a naked woman showing up in a man's cabin was likely to give the wrong impression.

Still, as with so many things, she counted on darkness, though she didn't hesitate to grab Ol' Yammer's shirt from where he'd left it draped over the back of a chair ready for morning and don it as a makeshift robe before reaching to gently touch his arm.

He woke quickly, probably wasn't even fully asleep yet. He didn't make any sound. Given the open door, he was probably used to creatures wandering in.

Though I doubt one as odd as I am, Prudence thought, strangling a laugh and instead saying softly, "Hush now, Yammer. I'm a friend. I've come to find if you want help getting out of here."

"Who?" His reply was hardly more than a breath. "How?"

"Prudence Bledsloe, don't think you'd recall…"

"I do. You had some interesting marks in your gun, as if you'd been firing silver bullets."

Prudence raised her eyebrows. *That* was a whole other tale, but true enough. He did remember her, then. "That's right. You want out of here?"

"Yes!"

"You watched?"

"Not so much, but checked on. And shackled." That last was said with a hiss of barely suppressed anger.

"If I got you out, you'd need to hide. The Oliver brothers have a lot of influence around here. Can you get to your tribe?"

A long sigh. "My 'tribe' is farther than you can imagine." Something in his inflection made Prudence keep her peace. As she'd hoped, he continued. "I am not Indian, as most think. I am from across the ocean."

"Chinese?" Prudence had met people from China before. Chinese men had been to the West since before the gold rush. Some had settled down. Others made their fortunes and went home again. Yammer had never struck her as Chinese, but then…

"No. I am from Nippon—Japan, as you would say it."

"Japan!" Prudence was astonished.

She'd heard of Japan, of course. It was supposed to be an exotic island nation, one that had sealed itself against all foreign influence until, sometime in the early '50's, the heroic Commodore Perry had convinced the rulers to open their ports to American vessels. Still, she'd gathered that the culture had remained resistant to foreign influence. What was a man from Japan doing here in California?

"My name is not Yammer," the man said. "It is Aoyama, Aoyama Daizaburou."

That was a real tongue twister, but Prudence was willing to give it a try. "I'm sorry Mr. Daizaburou, if I've been naming you wrong."

The chuckle that sounded in the darkness seemed completely inappropriate. She hadn't mauled the word *that* much.

"Aoyama is my family name. Like the Chinese, we give the family name first. However, even on the ship here, American tongues found it difficult. I did not mind being 'Ol' Yammer.' It was easier than always correcting."

"I get that," Prudence said. She realized something. Ol' Yammer—Aoyama—was talking so much because he was lonely. She wondered if he had much of anyone to talk to.

"So you don't have a tribe to get to," she said. "That'll be a problem."

"I *would* like to go home," Aoyama said, his tone unmistakably forlorn. "I was planning to do so when Jack Oliver took me captive. The brothers had been customers of mine for a long while, so I told them I would soon be closing shop. They mistakenly assumed that I was in need of custom and offered me full-time employment with them. I told them, no thank you, I was returning home. When they realized that likely no one would miss me, they decided to make me vanish."

Prudence didn't bother to correct his assumption that no one had missed him. What good would it do for Aoyama to learn that some of his neighbors had suspected harm had come to him, but had been too afraid to act?

"Well, if you want to get home, then we'll have to figure out how," she said. "Tell me everything about the set-up here."

Aoyama did. He was a smart man, methodical. His attention to details indicated that, shackled or not, he hadn't given up hope of escaping.

"I don't suppose you could use some of your tools to get those shackles off," Prudence asked, when he finished.

Aoyama shook his head and then, no doubt thinking she couldn't see the motion in the dark, clarified. "They're riveted on. I'd need a rasp or file, and they're careful to take any tools away from me when I'm done with work for the day. I tried to 'forget' to put a pair of pliers in once, just to see if they were keeping track…"

He trailed off. Prudence said, "They were. Fine. If I brought you tools, could you use them to thin down an edge, so it could be broken?"

"I could but how…"

"Better you don't ask. I should clear out before your guard comes around. I may be back tonight. May not, but I promise you this, I'll get you out of here—or if I can't, I'll find someone who can, someone who isn't beholden to the Oliver brothers."

"Why? Why do you care?"

Prudence shrugged, thinking of many things. "Let's just say I have a debt to pay off. Now, close your eyes…"

She slipped out of the shirt, into wolf, and out the door, then went to explore the areas that during the day would be quite busy but were now quiet as death. Here, where the paths were churned by humans and their animals, the faint tracks of her paws wouldn't show. She was getting hungry—shifting did that to her—so she raided the cookhouse, facing down a couple of sleepy old hounds who couldn't quite believe what they were seeing.

Then she went to the blacksmith's forge. The Oliver brothers might have kept tight control on Aoyama's tools, but they clearly didn't worry about the blacksmith's supplies. She was able to help herself to a nice assortment from a heap of older rasps and files, set aside as scrap. She dropped these with a startled Aoyama.

"Don't look for me tomorrow or even the next couple of days. I'm going to need to figure out how to get you clear, otherwise this is a waste of time. Work on the shackles but don't let anyone catch you at it."

"I will. If you have not returned in a month, I will know you cannot help me. However, with these I can remove the leg irons and take myself away."

Prudence knew this was his way of letting her off the hook. "Right. See you!"

***

She laid her groundwork carefully, even going so far as to let a hand from the Bar Nothing "walk out" with her so she had an excuse to take a good look at the Oliver compound by daylight. She didn't bother to ask questions about guards or anything that would raise suspicions. With what she had in mind, that wouldn't matter.

Her work at the shipping office made it easy to learn about ships heading to Japan. There were more than she'd expected, so she'd have her pick of ports, but first she needed to get him away.

Prudence waited for the full moon for two reasons. One was that, although half of what she'd heard about werewolves and full moons was nonsense, it was true that she was stronger when the moon was full. Unlike those who were "turned" rather than born, Prudence had no difficulties with self-control, but then she'd always taken her name and the self-control it implied very seriously.

The second was that Aoyama would benefit from having some light during the early stages of their escape. She wasn't worried that they'd be easier to spot. She already had plans to make sure that the Bar Nothing hands would be quite distracted.

A few days before, Prudence "quarreled" with her new beau, which gave her an excuse to quit her job and leave town, heading back toward New Mexico, or so she told folks. This let her take both Buck and Trick, as well as the better part of her belongings when it was time to go. She left early and said few goodbyes, before joining up with a wagon train heading east.

A few hours out, she had "second thoughts," and turned around for town. What she actually did was lay up in the hills and wait for night. The land she was on was poor land for grazing, so she expected to meet no one. Wolf form had enabled her to scout out a place to leave the horses out of sight but near at hand.

This time, she made the trek to Aoyama's cabin as a human. She found him awake and alert. "I thought you might be coming," he said as greeting. "There has been a fire."

Prudence crooked a small grin. "Funny that. They really shouldn't have stockpiled quite so much hay. Shackles?"

Aoyama showed her a spot he'd worn thin. "I can cut it through in…"

Prudence shook her head, knelt, and using the rasp as a lever, snapped the thinned metal. Aoyama didn't question, but stepped clear of the shackles as she slid the retraining bar out of its brackets.

"Can you run?" she asked, offering him an arm.

He didn't take it. "Without that weight, I can fly."

He was as good as his word. Later, as he was mounting up on Trick, he explained that he'd been doing all he could to get ready—including walking as much as possible to strengthen his legs. "I used putting in a second garden patch as an excuse. Pity I won't get to see the beans sprout."

They rode until dawn, then made camp well off the road. "I figure they're not going to be able to look for you too openly," Prudence said, "because that would take some explaining, since you weren't supposed to have been there, nor did they have any reason to keep you. Still, no need to make it easy."

Over the next few days, they travelled by night, camped when the roads were busy. Aoyama was eager to talk. As Prudence suspected, he'd been starved for companionship during his captivity.

"When you said you'd be rescuing me, I imagined something out of one of those dime novels, six guns blazing, posse gathered, sheriff holding out his star."

Prudence quirked the corner of her mouth in a smile. "That's fiction. In reality, when guns are blazing, lots of people get hurt who don't need to. I'd rather sacrifice a little cattle feed."

"I'm surprised to witness such restraint from an American," Aoyama said, "especially a lady who carries a pair of six guns and a rifle."

"I just use them to stay safe," she replied, not bothering to mention safe from what. "I heard that the Japanese didn't have guns until we brought them to you. Did you come here to learn gun-smithing?"

"What you heard is not precisely true," Aoyama said. "Japan has had firearms since the thirteenth century. During the Sengoku, what you might want to think of as our own war between the states—although there were a whole lot more states involved than just the North and South, and the wars lasted a great deal longer—many armies used matchlock rifles."

"Was this recently?"

"Oh, no, those wars belong to what you people call the 'Middle Ages.' They began in the mid-1460's and ended in 1573. Even before the Sengoku ended, those in charge realized that firearms upset the balance of power. It takes years to train someone to use a sword or bow—even a spear—with any skill. However, learning to use a rifle, especially for massed combat, takes weeks, maybe months."

Prudence's expression became wry. "So when you speak of the 'balance of power,' you mean keeping the power out of the hands of the masses? The British had a similar thought when they were in charge over here, but we Americans weren't having any of that. That's why our Constitution asserts the right to bear arms."

Aoyama did not disagree. "But your land was a frontier, even then, with Indians and competing colonial powers. As I understand your history, many people also relied on hunting and felt they needed guns to control predators. Japan, by contrast, was a single people. Our wildlife problems were not as extreme. Although some of the peasantry did try to rise up, there were many others who wished for wars to be over and a return to more settled times."

"So you—or rather those long-ago Japanese—just stopped using guns?"

"Not completely. If there was a need for pest control, guns could be rented, even by commoners, but in the absence of large-scale war, with contact with the outside world restricted to one port, swords, bows, spears were enough to maintain order."

Prudence cocked her head. "Were you already a gunsmith before you came here, or did you come here to learn?"

"My family is of samurai lineage—the warrior class who support the ruler. In the centuries following the Sengoku, there was a need to find professions other than fighting. Many samurai became administrators. My family clung to the warrior tradition and became gunsmiths."

"I guess I can see that. Can't have made you a lot of money, though, if most people couldn't have guns."

"No, it didn't. Sometimes we resented this, for we were artists and wished to have our art appreciated. It is probably unpatriotic of me to admit this but, in 1853, when Commodore Perry came in with his gun boats and forced the shogun and his associates to capitulate, I was actually delighted. My first thought was 'So, how do you feel when someone else holds a weapon over your heads and tells you what you may or may not do?' Now though, now that I have seen the rule of the gun here in America, I prefer our way. I wish we could go back, even though my trade was severely restricted and my family remained poor. I pray that even as Japan reintroduces firearms, we keep them under control."

"I guess I can see your point, but it's pretty hard to go back, isn't it?"

Aoyama coughed a dry, humorless laugh. "Oh, yes. Your Commodore Perry may not have realized what he was doing when he forced those who ruled Japan to open our ports to foreign trade. My understanding is that Perry—and Americans in general—think of Japan as a backward nation. That is why he felt he could threaten as he did. Did you know he said he would use his ships' guns to destroy Edo, our capital city, if we did not capitulate to his demands?"

Prudence frowned. "I heard something like that but, I admit, you make what he did sound more like bullying, instead of heroic decisiveness. Mr. Aoyama, I hope you won't get angry at me for asking this, but when you said that we Americans think of Japan as backward, well, aren't you? I mean, where things like guns are concerned."

"Perhaps," Aoyama's smile was a little sad, "we were in 1853, but we are very good at adapting. Japan is quite different from the other little island nations that the Europeans and Americans have found easy to dominate because you have guns and the islanders do not. We may have given up the gun, but we never gave up the culture of war. I believe that a time will come when America will regret humiliating our rulers. They will not forget. Generations will pass, but Japan will not forget. War is not something made by weapons, it is made within the mind."

Prudence, thinking of what it was to have fangs, but not to use them, to be a hunter, but not necessarily a killer, understood. Recalling how very fine Aoyama's guns were, how quickly he had adapted to the models favored by Americans, and how he had even improved on them, she wondered just what she was helping get home.

But help him get home she would, because she'd promised, and because holding back one drop would not turn back the flood that others had set into motion.

***

Some days later, they stood on the docks, saying their goodbyes. Over the time they'd travelled together, Prudence had come to think maybe she wasn't doing a bad thing sending Aoyama home. His skill would bring him to the attention of those in power, and his experiences might shape the decisions they would make.

Aoyama had been all but counting down the hours to his ship's departure, so Prudence was somewhat surprised to see him delay when the boarding process began. Instead, he stood, shuffling his feet slightly, holding his travel bag in front of him with both hands.

"You have been a good friend to me, Miss Bledsloe," Aoyama said, "and I should greatly dislike to replay kindness with discourtesy, but I have a question for you."

For a moment, Prudence thought he might be about to propose marriage, but that would be ridiculous. Startled, she gave a slight nod.

"Are you a *kitsune*?"

"What?"

"In Japan we have legends of women who can turn into foxes. Sometimes they are malicious tricksters, but sometimes they take a fancy to a man and come to his aid. I was wondering if you were a *kitsune*. On that first night when you came to my cabin, you told me to close my eyes, but I did not. I saw you become a creature that might be a fox, although larger... But so many things are larger here than they are at home, so I thought that foxes could be as well."

Prudence nearly laughed from astonishment, but she knew that would hurt Aoyama, make him believe he'd insulted her as he had feared. Instead she shrugged. Why not tell the truth? They'd never meet again and even if he did tell, no one would believe him. He'd just feed the rumor she already cultivated.

"I'm not a *kitsune*, but your eyes weren't lying. My family has shapeshifter blood and I can become a wolf."

"*Okami*, then," he said. "Fitting for one who comes to the aid of near strangers."

"What do you mean?"

"Written one way, *okami* means 'wolf,' but written another way, it means *great spirit*. I think it takes a very great spirit indeed to refrain from using power to harm, to use it instead to help. That is an omen, one I will remember when I go home and begin to make guns for my nation."

"Do that," Prudence said, feeling her belly warm with pleasure. "I'd like that. I'd like that very much, indeed."

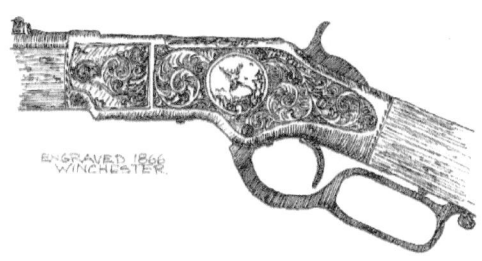

The Gift of a Gun

A Story of Teddy Roosevelt

Frances Bonney Jenner

"...and let them have dominion over the fish of the sea, and over the fowl of the air, and over the cattle, and over all the earth..." Genesis

No one could have seen it coming. Not even the birds on the River Nile in Egypt, especially the birds.

The boy, Teddy Roosevelt, called Teedie as a child, received the gift the summer of 1872, when he was 13 years old.

And it wasn't expected, this gift, especially not from Teddy's father, Theodore, Teddy's beloved role model.

As the son of a wealthy and prominent New York businessman, Theodore had turned his passion and attention to philanthropy. Together with pioneer social worker Charles Loring Brace, Theodore established the Children's Aid Society to provide for the 20,000 homeless children of New York City, called "street rats." Next came the Newsboys Lodging House on West 18th Street that offered several hundred newsboys a clean bed and warm room, all for an affordable 5 cents.

Touched by the hardships of others, the chestnut-bearded and big-bodied Theodore spent Sundays at the house and he became acquainted with each boy. Called Greatheart by his family, he gave the stray news-boys his time, his affection, his sympathy and often inspired them to seek a new direction. His friend Brace said of Theodore, "You felt the moment Mr. Roosevelt was in the room that he was a help to those poor fellows."

And he gave the same to his four children, his daughters Bamie and Corinne and sons, Teddy and Elliott. When home, they had his undivided attention. Each day Teddy and his siblings began the morning with Theodore in their five-story brownstone on 28 East 20th Street in Manhattan. He sat them down on the sofa in their home library and gathered them closely together. All four would bow their heads and pray with Theodore. The children greeted him when he arrived home from work and would accompany him up the long stairs to watch him dress in a beautifully tailored and styled suit as he prepared for dinner. He taught them to ride horses, climb trees and he took them to the Lodging House with him on Sundays.

Perhaps the idea of the gift somehow came from his mother's side of the family. Teddy adored his mother, Mittie, a great-spirited southern beauty from the Bulloch family of Roswell, Georgia. Mittie was a gifted storyteller and she filled their Manhattan brownstone with her wit and charm, spinning romantic tales of her daring ancestors and portraying the men in her family as great heroes and men of action.

James Dunwoody Bulloch, her older half-brother and a Confederate Admiral, carried out secret missions in England during the Civil War. He secretly arranged for the famous Confederate raider war sloop, the Alabama, to be built. Irvine Bulloch, Mittie's younger brother, served on the Alabama and in the Alabama's last battle with the Union sloop Kearsarge, Irvine is said to have fired the last two shots, despite defeat. Mittie's grandfather Stewart, a Revolutionary War general, left Georgia to fight Indians in Florida with his six sons, all over 6 feet tall. Impressionable Teddy remembered in his diaries the stories of Georgia bear hunts and men wrestling with bears and cougars, only to have their scalp torn away or be killed. Stories of guns and violence and death "made an indelible impression," remembered Teddy's sister Bamie.

Ironically it was these tales that sometimes calmed Teddy during his asthma attacks. Teddy's asthma surfaced when he was three years old. He experienced severe attacks and they had a devastating affect on the whole family. Often plans had to be changed and commitments cancelled. When traveling, Mittie or Theodore might have to move Teddy to a new locale, to Saratoga or Oyster Bay, a summer hotel at Richfield Springs, or back home to Manhattan to ease the attack. In January, 1868, Teddy was so ill that Mittie took him to her half-sister's home in Philadelphia to be treated by her husband, Hilbourne West, a physician.

Teddy slept sitting up in bed or in a big chair since it was so difficult for him to breathe. The attacks usually happened early in the morning around 4 am. As Teddy struggled for breath, Theodore would take him in his arms and walk him up and down the brownstone stair steps, in and out of the big rooms, and through the hallways that led from one room to another. Theodore walked him throughout the night and for hours on end.

And during the more difficult nights, Theodore would summon the servants to prepare the horses and carriage. He would take Teddy out, place him in the carriage, and Theodore and Teddy would ride into the dark and often cold nights. The clip-clopping of their two perfectly matched carriage horses would break silence as they trotted under the old Elm trees and along the streets of nearby Central Park, the moon and stars visibly overhead. Sometimes this sudden change of air and scenery worked to relieve the attack.

In an attempt to prevent the attacks, Theodore consulted with doctors who advised Teddy to build up his scrawny and underweight body. Theodore called Teddy to his side and said to him, "You must make your body. It is hard drudgery to make one's body, but I know you will do it." Mittie took him dutifully to the gymnasium where he did daily workouts with dumbbells and weights and punching bags. "Get action" was Theodore's mantra for Teddy and all his family.

The family traveled abroad in 1869. An English doctor's prescription for Teddy advised him to be "in a pure and bracing air… under a bright sky "and that would be a better cure for him than any medicine. Theodore and Teddy hiked up Castle Hill, a castle ruin from Saxon times, in the town of Hastings, a small English seaside village. In Switzerland, the whole family hiked astonishing numbers of miles. Teddy accompanied Theodore19 miles up the Tete-Noire and 20 miles across the Grimsel with an altitude of 7000 feet. In August of '71, Theodore took the whole family to the Adirondacks, Teddy's first wilderness experience roughing it, and then onto the White Mountains where Teddy and Elliott climbed Mount Lafayette. In Teddy's journal for that month there was no mention of asthma.

During the summers of 1871-'72, Theodore rented summer homes along the Hudson, and to his delight, Teddy replaced his gymnasium workouts (which he considered drudgery) with swimming, riding, and running barefoot through the open fields. "I am to do everything for myself," Teddy wrote in his journal, after spending a long day with his father.

And it was that summer of '72 that Theodore presented Teddy with the gift, despite Theodore being neither gunman nor hunter. The gift was a 12 gauge, double-barreled French Lefaucheux shotgun with a good kick to it, a perfect gun for the gawky 13 year old Teedie.

In the fall of October, 1872, the family set out for a trip to Egypt where they spent the winter traveling along the Nile. Teddy took his new gun along and by mid-December he was rambling along the banks of the Nile and happily whacking birds out of the sky at an astounding pace.

All kinds of birds winter along the Nile, larks, doves, herons, hawks and ibises. Teddy observed as many as 15 species. He wrote in his journal of being near Cairo at sundown where he saw ibises roosting on trees "whitened with immense multitudes." At that time Teddy considered himself to be a naturalist. He kept pet mice in his bureau drawer and had collected animal specimens (dead salamanders, mice, red squirrels, and even the skull of a beached whale) since he was seven years old. He placed his several hundred specimens in the Roosevelt Museum of Natural History, located in the back hall on the fourth floor of their home. And he learned the art of taxidermy from John G. Bell, who had stuffed all of Audubon's bird specimens.

As a self-proclaimed naturalist, Teddy felt compelled to collect birds when his family sailed south on the houseboat Theodore had chartered for the journey up the Nile. Thus began the killing. Teddy wandered daily along the river shores plunging through bogs or riding a little donkey, his big gun slung over his shoulder. He killed larks and doves and a pelican and even an ibis. The number of birds shot during the two months along the Nile amounted to between 100 and 200. Teddy lost count. He never knew for sure.

For that Christmas of '72, he received another shotgun, even more powerful than his original Lefaucheux. Using it, he could kill five starlings with a single shot. Teddy took so much pleasure in the hunting that even Theodore got into the spirit. And this was new for Theodore, who previously had saved a yellow jacket stuck in a pot of honey, holding it gently in his hands, until he let it go freely. In his journal entry, Teddy wrote "Father and I went out shooting and procured eighteen birds."

In a letter to her sister, Mittie wrote of Teddy's "eyes sparkling with delight" when he came to her holding a dead crane, the biggest bird he had killed. Perhaps the power of the gun was a relief for a boy afraid that every breath might be his last. And during the Nile river trip, some-how, Teddy's asthma took leave again.

After each day's hunt Teddy would bring his game bag back to the houseboat, spread out his kill and taxidermy kit, and proceed to skin and gut each bird, then pull the skin back over the bird's skull, for keeping. This required great patience and skill and often members of the crew, other guests, and family watched the performance. Once while skinning a kestral, he found the remains of a lark, a lizard and some beetles and, of course, being a naturalist at heart, this discovery thrilled him. Apparently the smell of the kill and the gutting and Teddy's body odor were all mixed up into a most unpleasant odor and Bamie remembered that Teddy's new passion was "to the discomfort of everyone connected with him."

Teddy never stopped hunting.

He hunted while a Harvard undergraduate student, a Columbia law student, and as he began and continued his political career. The August after graduating from Harvard, Teddy and his brother Elliott sojourned together on a hunting trip to Illinois, Iowa and Minnesota. They considered it their last chance for an adventure since Teddy planned to marry in October. They managed to kill in excess of 400 birds, grouse, geese, snipes, plovers, ducks and grebes, but described the hunt as "not as good as expected," most probably because they hunted on foot rather than riding over the prairie on great steeds that raced like the wind. That was Teddy's idea of the real west and he longed for the adventure of it.

Teddy married Alice Lee, the love of his life, in the fall of 1880, just months after his graduation. Two years prior while still at Harvard, Teddy had lost his father from stomach cancer. And tragically, on Valentines Day of '84, Mittie died unexpectedly from typhoid fever. Eleven hours later Alice died from an undiagnosed kidney ailment (Bright's Disease). She died as she lay in Teddy's arms, his Alice, dead at 22. Just two days before her death she had birthed their first child, a daughter, also named Alice. In his memorial to Alice written later that year Teddy wrote, "And when my heart's dearest died, the light went out from my life forever."

Perhaps Teddy's overwhelming grief and his unimaginable losses spurred him to abandon politics, to entrust the rearing of his daughter Alice to his sister Bamie, to never to speak of Alice again, and to turn to his new interest, the Dakota Badlands.

He had first gone west to the Badlands in1883 to hunt buffalo. He and his guide Joe Ferris tracked buffalo for several days as they traveled over wild and difficult terrain. Roosevelt set an exhausting pace. They found buffalo twice and each time Teddy shot and missed. It rained constantly and for two days they had only biscuits and water for sustenance. Ferris prayed Teddy would give up and said of him, "You just couldn't knock him out of sorts." When Roosevelt finally shot his buffalo on the other side of the Montana line, according to Ferris he danced his own wildly enthusiastic version of an Indian war dance and gave Ferris 100 dollars. Ferris said, "I never saw anyone so pleased in my life."

Roosevelt invested in cattle ranching in the Badlands between 1883-86 and even partnered in having a small ranch house built. After Alice's death, he spent as much time there as possible, traveling often between New York and the Dakota territory. The Badlands gave him a place to go to be away from the public eye so that he was able to grieve privately. He became a cowboy there, riding his horses and herding cattle. He was living the authentic ranch life that had summoned him. He wrote in 1884, "... not even at sea does a man feel more lonely than when riding over the far reaching, seemingly never-ending plains; and after a man has lived a little while on or near them, their very vastness and loneliness and their melancholy monotony have a strong fascination for him...Nowhere else does one seem so far off from all mankind...."

He immersed himself, too, in being a hunter, as he was living on the land amidst deer and antelope, buffalo and bighorn sheep, and magpies and meadowlarks. His lever-action 45-75 Winchester (Model 1976) had been custom made for his specific needs and was engraved with antelope, deer, and buffalo, "the best weapon I ever had," he said. Roosevelt had not taken such pleasure in owning a gun since the first gun his father gave him.

During a two-month fall hunting expedition to the Big Horns in Wyoming at that time he took his prize gun, killed his first grizzly bear, and hunted every day, pushing himself to his physical limits to kill quantities of prairie chickens, sage hens, doves, rabbits—over 100 birds and small game—and also elk and deer.

As a naturalist, Roosevelt had a profound sensitivity to the wild beauty of the animals that he killed and yet as a hunter that sensibility was coupled with a powerful lust for killing any animal he wished. He said of the black tail buck that he shot during the trip, "Every movement is full of alert, fiery life and grace, and he steps as lightly as though he hardly trod the earth." Upon killing the "best" elk of the trip, he reminisced that when he heard the magnificent bugling of an elk it was, "impossible to believe that it is the call of the animal."

As part of the hunting trip, he and his friend Bill Merrifield packed up to 9000 feet into the mountains along Ten Sleep Creek when they began tracking a sought-after grizzly into a thicket. The bear left its claw marks on fallen trees and broken twigs. They followed and came upon the "monstrous" bear, nine feet tall, settled in among a group of small Spruce trees, and some twenty feet in the distance. The grizzly reared up and then came down on all fours. Roosevelt later told Bamie, "I found myself face to face with the great bear, ... I could see the top of the bead fairly between his two sinister-looking eyes; as I pulled the trigger I jumped aside out of the smoke, to be ready if he charged, but it was needless, … the bullet hole in his skull was exactly between his eyes as if I had measured the distance with a carpenter's rule."

By 1886, Roosevelt sold his investments in the Badlands cattle ranching business and at a loss. The winter had killed off his cattle, he had grieved enough, and he was ready to return to his political and public life in New York. The three years of ranching and hunting in the Badlands had altered him physically. His ranch partner said of him, "When he got back into the world again, he was as husky as any man I have ever seen who wasn't dependent on his arms for a livelihood. He weighed 150 pounds and was clear bone, muscle and grit."

Roosevelt's love of the hunt continued throughout his life. His brother Elliot had traveled to India in 1880. There he had an opportunity to hunt big game. He wrote to Teddy about his hunt of one of the largest tigers in the area of the country, "Three hours after the blood had been running, she weighed 280 pounds…." and when she charged her final charge, he "finished her… (*the glorious brute*) with a spare shot from the Bone Crusher - by George, what a hole that gun makes." Upon receiving Elliott's letters about his tiger hunt, Mittie wrote to Elliott, "Poor dear Teddy …. longs to be with you and walks up and down the room…."

It is not surprising then that when Roosevelt retired from his presidency in 1909 that he set out for Africa to hunt big game. He made arrangements to collect African specimens for The Smithsonian Institution and The American Museum of Natural History. He traveled with his son Kermit and 250 porters and guides, across British East Africa (now Kenya) into the Belgian Congo (now The Democratic Republic of the Congo) and back to the Nile ending in Khartoum (now Sudan). The expedition collected 11,397 specimens, "the most notewor-thy collection of big animals that has ever come out of Africa," Roosevelt said. He brought with him his Winchester 405 rifle, a double-barreled shotgun, and an Army Springfield, a military bolt-action rifle, the most powerful weapon used at that time, with an aim to kill as many big-game Safari animals as he could. Roosevelt killed 296 large animals, including 15 zebras, 13 rhinoceroses, 8 elephants, 9 lions, 8 warthogs, a crocodile, 5 wildebeests, 6 monkeys, 2 ostriches and 3 pythons. Between the two of them, Kermit and Teddy killed 512 animals.

Roosevelt wrote about his Safari travels in his serialized account titled *African Game Trails: An Account of the African Wanderings of an American Hunter-Naturalist* published by Charles Scribner's Sons. Francis A. Collins wrote of the publication in his *New York Times* review, "The object of Mr. Roosevelt's African expedition, it is explained repeatedly, was purely scientific. It was undertaken primarily to collect birds, mammals, reptiles, and plants, and especially big game for the National Museum at Washington and the Natural History Museum of New York. No game of any kind was shot except for scientific purposes or for food."

Also interviewed by the *New York Times*, nature writer Dr. William J. Long spoke of: "The brutalizing influence which these reports (serials) have upon thousands of American boys. Only last week I met half a dozen little fellows in the woods. The biggest boy had a gun and a squirrel's tail in his hat, and he called himself Bwana Tumbo. They were shooting everything in sight." He continued, "Is not the great American hero (Roosevelt) occupied at this time with the same detestable business?"

Roosevelt's description of his African rhino hunt shows the 19th century cultural sentiment and thinking regarding wildlife and nature that Roosevelt also shared and expressed. "The big beast stood like an uncouth statue, his hide black in the sunlight: he seemed what he was, a monster surviving over from the world's past, from the days when the beasts of the prime ran riot in their strength, before man grew so cunning of brain and hand as to master them."

These cultural values of the time, that man not only had the right but also the duty to dominate and conquer the natural world, had resulted in four million bison being slaughtered in the latter 1800's. Hide hunters killed up to 250 bison a day to satisfy the need for buffalo coats and tongue, a delicacy sold in restaurants. Sport hunters shot buffalo from trains as buffalo crossed the railroad tracks. The U.S. army encouraged the slaughter as a way to control the Native American populations who depended on the buffalo for survival. Army General Philip Sheridan said, "Let them kill, skin, and sell until the buffalo is exterminated, as it is the only way to bring lasting peace and allow the civilization to advance."

By 1890 the number of American bison was less than 1000. The passenger pigeon had been hunted out of existence by the early 1900's as well, by sport and professional hunters, with no attempt to save the species.

Considering Roosevelt's hunting practices that fell in line with the cultural attitudes of the day, it seems contradictory or at least ironic that he was considered a conservationist. He killed savagely and yet concerned himself with saving critical habitats and remaining populations of wildlife. Troubled by the slaughter of the buffalo, he used his presidential pulpit to create public support for wildlife and a conservation ethic.

As President, Roosevelt provided federal protection for almost 230 million acres of land. He set aside 150 national forests, the first 51 federal bird reserves, five national parks, 18 national monuments, the first four national game preserves, and the first 24 reclamation projects that were bitterly opposed by commercial interests. Roosevelt wrote, "It is also vandalism wantonly to destroy or to permit the destruction of what is beautiful in nature, whether it be a cliff, a forest, or a species of mammal or bird."

Late nineteenth and early twentieth century conservationists held the belief that preserving wildlife habitats did not mean keeping humans out in order to protect the habitat but rather allowing humans in to use the land freely for any natural resource that could benefit them. Roosevelt could as easily use his Winchester to hunt down any animal he pleased as he could pen a national park or federal game preserve.

And Roosevelt became an advocate for hunting on the lands he sought to protect, as seen in his writing from *The Wilderness Hunter*, "In hunting, the finding and killing of the game is after all but a part of the whole. The free, self-reliant, adventurous life, with its rugged and stalwart democracy; the wild surroundings, the grand beauty of the scenery, the chance to study the ways and habits of the woodland creatures—all these unite to give to the career of the wilderness hunter its peculiar charm. The chase is among the best of all national pastimes; it cultivates that vigorous manliness for the lack of which in a nation, as in an individual, the possession of no other qualities can possibly atone."

Just one action can often determine an unpredictable and extraordinary result. Theodore's gift of a shotgun to his son Teddy changed everything, for Teddy, for the nation, for the future.

The boy was Teddy Roosevelt, a naturalist turned hunter, who killed birds and animals by the hundreds and perhaps thousands, and yet became the conservation President.

He killed the doves and ibises along the Nile, the buffalo and bear of the Badlands, the lions, zebras, and rhinos of Africa.

He killed them all, the conservation President did, and yet he saved millions of acres of America's natural lands.

Teddy's sister, Corinne tells the story of walking outside the White House with Teddy one spring morning. He stopped and suddenly bent down to grab a tiny feather from the ground. He held it gingerly between his thumb and index finger, and said "Very early for a fox sparrow."

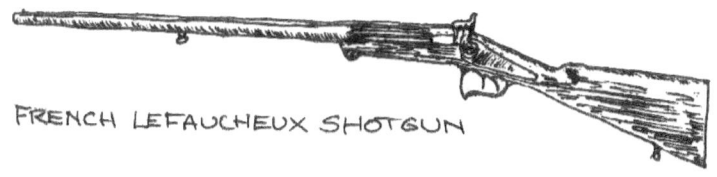

FRENCH LEFAUCHEUX SHOTGUN

The Assassination of Reinhard Heydrich

Jan Wiener

Despite his complete absorption, a document on Heydrich's desk caught his notice. This paper set forth Heydrich's complete personal schedule for May 27, hour by hour. Novotny was startled to observe that the day's activities included the Reichsprotector's permanent departure from Prague, by plane, on the afternoon of that day.

Seizing a moment when Heydrich had left the room, Novotny snatched this paper from the desk, crumpled it up, and threw it into the wastebasket before Heydrich returned. Then, satisfying himself that the clock and its chimes were performing in good order, he left.

Minutes later, a cleaning woman, Marie Rasnerova, entered the office and dutifully emptied the wastebasket for the Reichsprotector's convenience, without in the least disturbing him as he worked at his desk. The crumpled paper then speedily made its way through channels—to Vanek, to Zelenka, to Kubish and Gabchik.

Both Vanek and Zelenka were delighted to pass on this document which pinned down the day and hour of the hated Heydrich's departure. It is probable that they both hoped that the assassination could now be abandoned. However, Kubish and Gabchik interpreted the information quite differently. The morning of May 27 became their absolute deadline.

Gabchik's Sten gun would be the murder weapon. Kubish's bomb would be used as back-up, if necessary. Both would wear pistols concealed in shoulder holsters, to be used, if needed, for defense.

Both Gabchick and Kubish would be riding women's bicycles; but since bicycles were in short supply, this would not be incongruous. The battered briefcases they both would carry would also be too common to be noticed. One of the few privileges left to Czechs was the freedom to raise rabbits for food; a briefcase in which to carry grass for one's rabbits was frequently carried, even within city limits. In fact the briefcase found for Gabchik had been in use for this purpose until the day it reached his hands. The Sten gun would be carried disassembled; the bomb would be ready. At the Moravech apartment Kubish carefully went over its workings with Atya, to be sure that it was in order.

The morning of May 27 dawned bright and clear—a good sign, as Heydrich would undoubtedly ride in his open car to enjoy the beautiful sunshine. Kubish and Gabchik, in their separate hideouts, both arose with the birds, in cheery moods typical of young men on a bright spring day. Kubish, quartered in the Ogoun apartment, stopped to cheer Professor Ogoun's young son who was cramming for an exam.

"Don't worry, Lubos," he said. "You'll pass it easily, and tonight we'll celebrate together." Young Lubos, concerned with his own forthcoming ordeal, did not ask what Kubish expected to celebrate.

Opalka staying with Mrs. Teresa Sojkova, also rose early that morning. He dressed carefully, inspecting the contents of his pockets, and took his pistol from its hiding place. He said goodbye as usual to Mrs. Sojkova and to Alenka, her little daughter, who knew him as Uncle Opalka.

"This will be a busy day," he said. "If I'm not back by eight o'clock tonight, I won't be home, so don't worry." Waving, he ran down the stairs and out to the street to catch his usual streetcar.

According to prearranged plan, the paratroopers went separately to a meeting place in the Vysocany sector of Prague, where they joined waiting members of the underground including Zelenka and Rela Fafek. Here each of the helpers was assigned a battle station. Rela was dispatched to get her car and her Easter bonnet and to wait for Heydrich at the outskirts of Prague. Valchik, equipped with a hand mirror, was posted at the bend in the road to signal the approach of the target by refracting the sun's rays. The others mingled with the street population to become passers-by along the route, ready to distract or engage the police if necessary.

Gabchik and Kubish rode on beyond the bend and parked their bicycles at the chosen spot. Gabchik removed his raincoat and slung it over his arm. Five months' worth of careful planning were about to reach their culmination.

If all went as planned, Gabchik would shoot both Heydrich and his driver with the Sten gun, then ride away; Kubish would snatch Heydrich's briefcase, doubtless full of strategic information of use to London, and would substitute his own case which contained his bomb at the ready. Then he too would ride away. They would make their escapes independently and would lie low in separate hideouts until it seemed safe to make contact.

Each carrying his briefcase, the two ambled to their posts, a few feet apart, every motion premeditated. They assumed their accustomed pose of casual loiterers. Opalka slouched nonchalantly in a nearby doorway, ready to do what might be needed to cover their escape.

The spot beyond the bend had been selected because the road curved sharply at that point, forcing a driver to brake his car and to make the turn slowly. It was a blind turn in both directions. They waited for the prearranged signals to tell them what to expect.

At 10:31 Rela Fafek drove slowly around the corner in her rented car, bareheaded.

Gabchik smoothly assembled his Sten gun with one hand without removing it from the briefcase. Then, discarding the briefcase, he hid the gun under his coat.

Seconds later Valchik's signal came—the bright, restless flashes from the mirror. Gabchik now dropped his coat and stepped into the

81

road. He aimed at the bend around which the open Mercedes soon appeared, taking the curve carefully. The target was perfect. The aim was perfect. He pulled the trigger.

He pulled it again. Nothing happened.

The gun was jammed. A shred of grass from the briefcase had canceled out all the planning.

Kubish, tense and ready, leaped into action. As both Heydrich and his chauffeur drew their pistols to shoot him down, Kubish reached into his briefcase, withdrew the bomb, and hurled it toward Heydrich, who was now standing up in the car aiming at the stunned Gabchik.

The bomb exploded near the car's rear wheel, shattering the door. Heydrich, wounded and immobilized, dropped his pistol. Fragments of exploding debris hit Kubish in the face, but despite impaired vision he managed to jump on his bicycle and pedal away, bleeding profusely.

Gabchik, starting to run, dropped his useless gun, drew his shoulder pistol, and shot the now pursuing chauffeur in both legs. Then he too escaped. Heydrich was still standing upright, probably in shock, waiting for help to come. But he found himself surrounded by stony-faced pedestrians who noticed nothing out of order.

One lone woman—a collaborator—recognizing Heydrich, turned in agitation to those around her, appealing for aid.

"It is Herr Heydrich!" she screamed. "Help him! Help him! It is the Reichsprotector!"

The unsympathetic passers-by made various sarcastic comments before they melted away. "The hospital is just around the corner," one suggested. "Let him walk!" A trolley lumbered around the bend; its driver and its passengers peered curiously but were not inclined to stop. Heydrich's lone sympathizer forced a truck to halt by blocking its path and demanded assistance from the driver.

The truck driver, noticing the SS uniform, apologized profusely and politely but explained that his truck was already too heavily loaded. He drove on.

Finally the woman succeeded in stopping a small station wagon; the driver of this car was willing to help the Reichsprotector. Heydrich tried to make the transfer from his own disabled car by himself, but he could not. When he tried to move, he collapsed. His two rescuers were forced to lift him, awkwardly and painfully, into the back of the car. They took him to the nearby hospital.

Kubish meanwhile pedaled furiously for a few blocks—past the hospital—to the nearest refuge that he knew of, the apartment of his friends the Novaks. Leaving his bicycle to slide to the ground in front of the building, he stumbled indoors.

Marie Novak washed his wounds and did what she could to stop the bleeding. She gave him clean clothes, her husband's railwayman's uniform, and disposed of the blood-soaked suit he had been wearing. While she was helping him, her fourteen-year-old daughter slipped outside and hid the bloodstained bicycle.

Disguised and burning to know how Gabchik had fared, Kubish followed Marie's urging and visited a resistance doctor who treated his badly wounded eye. Then, restless and anxious, he wandered the streets of Prague in search of a safe hiding place.

Gabchik was unhurt. He had escaped on foot to the Svatos home in the Old Town section, where he too changed clothes while listening to his own description blared from a street loudspeaker.

Heydrich was injured at about 10:33 on that morning. By eleven o'clock all Prague knew of the attack. But as yet Heydrich was still alive. After the first superficial examination by the doctor on duty, during which Heydrich sat upright and grim-lipped on the operating table, observing every move, he refused to be touched by any but a German doctor.

Later, X-rays revealed that bomb fragments had penetrated Heydrich's ribs. One rib was broken. His chest was damaged, and fragments were embedded in the pleura—the membrane between the ribs and lungs. Another fragment of the bomb was embedded in his spleen right under the rib basket and would have to be removed immediately.

A German doctor was now summoned from Berlin and more time passed. The operation was performed and the wound was found to be serious but not fatal. All Czechs except necessary nurses and attendants were excluded from Heydrich's room, which was actually an entire floor of the hospital. Machine guns were mounted on the roof and the whole building was thick with guards.

Heydrich seemed to be recovering as well as could be expected, so it was a complete surprise when suddenly on June 4, 1942, he died. Official announcement of the cause of death was infection from bacteria that had entered Heydrich's internal organs as a result of the explosive fragments. In other words, a bit of dirt had done him in.

What followed is both historically and widely known. Reprisals in the form of mass executions became a daily occurrence. Hitler himself selected the town of Lidice, a small mining village of a few hundred people, as the ultimate sacrifice. It was destroyed completely, the men executed, the women sent to camps, the children saved only if they were blue-eyed and blond haired.

None of the paratroopers survived. All seven were killed in the crypt of the Karel Boromaeus Greek Orthodox Church in Prague.

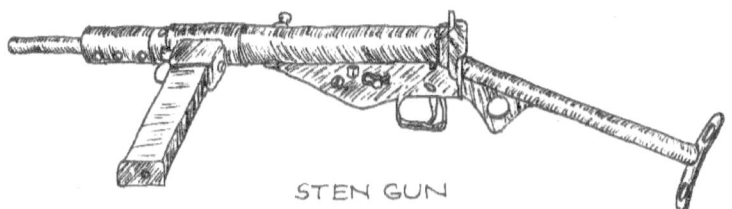

STEN GUN

The Day Something Happened

George Kolb

1940s

Mom honked the horn furiously, and I ran as fast as I could to our new 46 Hudson. As I got near I saw that her friend, Marguerite Thomas, was in the car with her.

Mom was crying and, as I opened the door, she said: "Something's happened."

"What?"

"Your dad killed Bogart. He's been charged with murder and released on bail."

Bogart was our next door neighbor. By this time, we'd sold our old house on Vance Jackson and built a new one in Oakland Estates, off Huebner Road on the south side of Fredericksburg Road. Anyway Bogart was a veteran alcoholic, who didn't work, stayed at home and drank whiskey. He often had drinking parties at his house. His wife worked hard to support the family.

Bogart had angered Dad by interrupting party line conversations my sisters had with their friends, sometimes using insulting sexual language and inferences.

Instead of confronting Bogart about this, Dad filed it away, but didn't forget.

"But why, Mom?" I asked.

"I was outside hanging out the wash. Bogart and his friends were having a drinking party next door. They started yelling at me to come over and join the party but I ignored them. Bogart then came over to the fence and yelled at me to come over, saying 'We see you strutting around over there.' I ignored him. Then he started through the fence, saying 'Ah, hell, I'll come get you.' I ran in the house, closed and locked all the doors, and called your dad. He raced home. By that time Pooch had chased Bogart back onto his own property.

"Your dad walked calmly into the house, picked up his 30-30 rifle and telephoned Bogart–'Meet me at the fence.' Then he walked out of the house and over to the fence with the rifle in his right hand, and I followed behind. When they met at the fence your dad said: 'You son of a bitch, you ever insult my wife or kids again and you will answer to this 30-30.'

"Bogart yelled back: 'Well, goddamn you, I'll stick that gun up your ass!' and he started through the fence, still cussing. Your dad pulled the trigger and with a huge gush of blood from his stomach, Bogart fell to the ground dead. Your dad then called the law and reported what had happened."

The next day the San Antonio paper published an article with the headline:

O. H. Kolb Faces Murder Charge

The kids at Horace Mann junior heard or read about it and asked me a lot of questions. Finally, our home room teacher instructed the entire class to not discuss or ask me any questions about it. I was in the room, sitting in my assigned seat, when she did that. I looked directly ahead the whole time, but could feel the stare of thirty three students, who were probably wondering if my dad was a bad person and whether they should hang out with me anymore. This bothered me a lot, but I was more worried about Dad.

Would he go to prison? Who would pay the bills? Could Mom get a job paying enough to cover that? She didn't even finish high school. My mind was whirling.

A week or more went by, after which Mom, Dad, and a Texas Ranger friend of Dad's, testified before the Grand Jury. The jury then retired, deliberated and returned a "No Bill" verdict. This meant that no charges would be prosecuted against Dad. So, he continued as manager of Ziegler Glass Company.

Dad was not the same after that. He drank more. He also became afflicted with severe rheumatoid arthritis in his hands. It soon became so bad that he could not even hold a small tack hammer. His fingers became misshaped, fanning out to the side. This condition is called "Swan's Wing" by doctors. It was not only debilitating, it was very painful and required strong medications, which made Dad groggy and his speech very slow and thick tongued. Eventually Dad had also developed arthritis in one of his knees. It was so severe that he underwent a surgical knee replacement. This became infected in the hospital requiring that his leg be amputated.

After this Dad slowly withdrew from life to his favorite chair, cigarettes, beer and TV. The last time I saw him he was living in an apartment with Mom and he was sitting in his favorite chair smoking cigarettes and drinking beer. He insisted that Mom was trying to kill him. I noted that within easy reach was the same butcher knife with aluminum handles, that I remembered so well.

In 1981 Dad died in a nursing home at the age of seventy nine. I recently did genealogy research on the Kolb family and found written accounts made by two of my now deceased aunts that Dad's grandmother had what appears to have been rheumatoid arthritis in her hands. It was described as so severe that she could not do her hair, clean the house, or prepare meals for her family and her teenage daughter had to do these things for her. So apparently Dad's condition was inherited.

Although Dad made some bad choices in his life, through it all I always felt very close to him. His family life growing up was much rougher than mine. I think about him often and miss him.

Dad's Beretta

From the memoir *TANGLED BYLINES,*
a father and son cover the twentieth century

Clyde H. Farnsworth

The center of my world was 50 Rockefeller Plaza, a skyscraper in Rockefeller Center, then a freshly rehabilitated 22-acre section of midtown between Fifth and Sixth Avenues. The AP was a charter leaseholder, having outgrown older digs on Madison Avenue. Fifty Rock and its sister towers, showcasing the latest in technology and design, hovered over gardens, sculptures, fountains, theaters, museums, restaurants, shops, even an ice-skating rink. The place still radiates chic and cool, confirming the initial vision.

I was nine.

Dad and I mostly traveled by subway, a longer ride than the New Haven Railroad commuter train, but cheaper. The "A" trolley ran behind our house. In twenty-five minutes, we were at 241st Street and White Plains Road, where we grabbed the Lexington Avenue Express. Fifty minutes later, Grand Central. Those days you rode to Coney Island for a nickel.

On the long ride from the northeast Bronx, I insisted we work our way to the lead car where I played engineer beside the real engineer's locked compartment. Other kids gravitated there as well, and we shoved for a good position. The best part of the ride was the long slide into the tunnel after Jackson Avenue under the silt and sand bed of the Harlem River. I worried about those tons of alluvial gunk and water overhead. "Relax!" Dad said, deep in Carl Sandburg's *Life of Lincoln*, or one of the many sections of the *Sunday Times*.

On at least one occasion he drove our old gray Studebaker into the city. Clusters of skyscrapers glistened in the morning haze as we crossed the Harlem River Bridge and swung into downtown Manhattan via Central Park, a site of murders and carjackings. At one red light, I asked if he were afraid. He smiled, opened the glove compartment, reached for something in a cloth—my first sight of the gun a Cleveland police captain slipped him as a memento. Cops and reporters used to butter each other up. Police impounded that gun from a local hood, and he probably shouldn't have kept it. "Our secret!" he said. "Don't tell your mother." I never did. I liked secrets. Years later, my kid brother came upon that gun in the linen closet. Ever resourceful Frank nearly lost a hand.

Though one of the coolest of men, Dad wasn't averse to packing heat—bravado he shared with other scribes of the day, some of whom carried guns openly. Growing up in rural Ohio, he accompanied his granddad on hunting and fishing trips. Bearing arms was as natural as picking apples by the oak-timbered barn at the Nankin crossroads.

In a Tegucigalpa marketplace years later he was offered a Beretta 9mm for $5. No bullets, just the gun itself, but as an admirer of Berettas, for "their fine machining," he couldn't resist, slipped it into a rucksack. He was awaiting a visa to enter Argentina, forgot about it until his Pan Am flight was to land in Buenos Aires. He'd left the AP by this time, and together with his new employer, Scripps Howard, was slamming Peron. Any airport incident would have been embarrassing, even job threatening. Where to put the Beretta?

Just before Fasten Seat Belts lights flashed, he rose, grabbed the knapsack, made for the lavatory. Locking the door, he extricated it, dropped it into the toilet. He flushed, and flushed, and flushed again until two pounds of sleek Italian steel slid on chutes of sweet-scented blue water into those Stygian depths. Recounting all this years later, eyes atwinkle, he added: "Don't cry for it, Argentina!"

BERETTA 9MM MODEL 92

The Valley Battle

Prelude

What is it about the Second World War that continues to grip us? Was it the last "good" war—when we were good and our adversaries unequivocally evil? Is it nostalgia for a hard-won victory after an all-out national effort? Do we wonder at this struggle that managed to touch each and every citizen, military and civilian alike?

All these factors play a part, for World War II continues to fascinate and intrigue Americans both young and old. Even the weapons of that conflict take on a certain romantic feel in comparison to modern, impersonal "smart" weapons and the world's nuclear arsenals. In the Second World War, weapons were lethal but not so advanced that individual skill and courage did not remain crucial to their success.

Growing up as a Chinese-American in middle America, I remember feeling a bit envious of friends who had a personal connection to the war. They had grandfathers who'd served. Their attics held treasures like old Army helmets or dog tags. Veterans Day held special meaning for them. In contrast, my grandfathers had never been soldiers. They'd not been touched by battles in Europe or the Pacific. Their lives had not been shattered by war.

Or had they?

It later dawned on me that the Japanese invasion of China had forced my grandfathers to flee their homeland, and that my own life in America was a direct result of the war. Though I pursued a career in medicine, I have never lost my fascination with China's role in the war. Tens of thousands of Americans served in China. Fifteen to twenty million Chinese died during the war. Many consider China to be WWII's "forgotten" theater, and I wanted to remedy this.

Andrew Lam

So I decided to write Two Sons of China.

Military action and weaponry play a significant role in my narrative. Some readers have asked why I wrote the battle scenes so graphically. I can only say that I wrote what I felt to be true. True to the fears and instincts of men who have seen combat up close, face to face with the enemy. As a surgeon, I know how messy real life can be. It's not storybook—not when life and death are at stake—I've seen tough, stoic men cry at the thought of getting a shot. I've seen petite elderly women endure the loss of a spouse without shedding a tear. There are some events so terrible, so painful or extraordinary, that many of us have no idea how we'll respond until it happens to us.

So it is with war. Marksmen miss their targets. Men suffer fear and even cowardice. Mortally wounded soldiers do not close their eyes and fall asleep, they cry for their mothers or suffer in silence or react in a multitude of other unpredictable ways.

Real life truly is stranger than fiction. That's what makes it real.

—Andrew Lam

The Valley Battle

From the novel *Two Sons of China*

Andrew Lam

Yuen stopped the group at the edge of a steep rise, the crest of a hill, many pine trees. While the others rested, he stared at the sudden change in the landscape.

It was a long, flat valley. The expanse stretched far to the north and south, lush and green. Across it, a half mile away, the land rose again, a chain of foothills running parallel to the range on which they stood. One straight, lonely road traversed the valley floor.

Yuen hesitated. Straight across would be the fastest, most direct route. *But also too exposed.* Looking left and right, there was no narrowing, no safer crossing. In fact, the valley opened up to a plain farther to the north. As far as he could see, the valley and road were empty.

He decided to lead the men straight across. There were sixteen of them left, thirteen Chinese and three Americans: Lieutenant David Parker who'd been with them since Yenan, and the two B-29 airmen they'd rescued, pilot Sam Masket and tail-gunner Billy. Captain Masket had broken leg—four Chinese carried him in a sedan chair.

The group descended the hill and emerged onto the soft valley floor. *More than soft*, Yuen thought. *This is from more than just rain—some kind of bog?*

Sunlight had yet to reach the base of the valley. Small groups of cattails grew in patches of shallow standing water. Knee-high sawgrass hid the sticky mud that sucked the soles of Yuen's shoes, slowing him. Three times he lifted his foot completely out of his shoe.

Yuen reached the road. *Halfway across.* The elevated roadbed was hard-packed dirt, the single lane straight and dusty. He glanced up and down its length. *No one in sight.*

He looked back. The sedan chair carrying Captain Masket had fallen behind. *We've got to get moving.* He took another close look at the road and saw fresh tire tracks, several of them.

This road is well traveled.

Suddenly, his eye caught sight of a quick-moving shadow gliding across the ground. Yuen's head jerked upward, a sense of dread in his gut.

He squinted at the sky.

Nothing.

A reddish hawk floated overhead.

Yuen exhaled slowly.

"Come on, let's get across." He singled out one of his men. "Jou, please give them a hand," he said, pointing to the men straining under the B-29 pilot's weight.

The sedan chair finally reached the road, which they crossed, and the whole entourage descended the short but steeply banked roadside, continuing west. Grasses around them bowed to gusts of wind, which rolled down the long axis of the valley. The rustling sound was pleasant, and it was easy to picture the men wading through a sea of grass. Yuen observed they were halfway between the road and the wooded foothills ahead.

Then, a sudden shout. Jou's voice, high pitched, alarmed.

"Japanese!"

Yuen spun and saw a convoy of two troop trucks and a jeep in the distance, coming from the north. A plume of dust kicked up behind the vehicles. The trucks sped up.

"Run!" Yuen shouted.

They would not reach the tree line in time. The Communists sludged across the muddy ground, stumbling and cursing while trying to crouch low. Behind them, the trucks skidded to a stop. Two dozen soldiers clambered out, bayonets affixed to their bolt-action Arisaka rifles.

Yuen stopped. The trees ahead were tantalizingly close. Thirty yards, maybe less, and Yuen was closer than anyone.

He looked back. *We're spread all over the place. No cover. Where's the sedan chair? Dammit! Get moving!*

Still forty yards back, the chair was an easy target. Yuen looked past it to the enemy soldiers bobbing through the boggy ground with speed that surprised him.

Have to make a stand. Yuen spread his arms out, barked orders.

"Stop! Stop! Form a line, covering fire!"

The men obeyed, dropping into the grass behind a few small boulders. Steady fire began. Enemy soldiers dove into the grass; some were hit.

"Keep it up!" Yuen shouted. He squeezed off two bursts with his Soviet-made PPS-43 submachine gun. By the gun's weight, he knew the 35-round magazine was probably half empty. Smoke in the air; the steady sound of the Browning Automatic Rifle off to the side.

"Get down!" a voice bellowed at him—Bao, the husky ox of a man, carrying the sedan chair with the others, straining, running. "Keep going with the American!" Bao hollered, now stopping to turn and join the fight. Jou grunted, unslung his M-1 Garand and handed it to Yuen before stumbling onward with the others.

Zip! Zhap!

Bullets incoming, zinging, cutting grass. Yuen flinched. A bullet hit nearby rock. He peered through the smoke and saw the enemy scrambling forward one by one in isolated spurts.

The young one. Yuen searched for Billy, the downed B-29's tail gunner, saw him behind a rock shooting his Colt pistol. Yuen ran to him, crouching low. He pulled Billy's shoulder.

Billy looked up, surprised, fright in his eyes, his pistol barrel smoking. Yuen jerked his thumb to the woods. *Go on, get back.*

Billy ran for the trees.

Yuen scanned the battle line. The Chinese were using the M-1s with accuracy. A soldier beside Yuen fired steadily: one, two, three, four shots—*clink!*

The clip ejected. Yuen saw two Japanese fall, then another. Somehow they seemed to be moving in slow motion.

Now THEY'RE stuck in the mud! Yuen thought.

The soldier jammed another clip in, took aim, then cursed: "Ma de! Zhong danle!"

He fell back, shot in the arm.

Yuen ducked. *Where's David? I've got to get him out of here too.* He looked, peering through the smoke. *Where is he?*

Finally Yuen saw him, his brown hair barely visible above the grasses, lying prone with the bulky Browning Automatic Rifle at the other end of the line, its repetitive sound deep, thumping. *Too far. He's on his own.* Yuen did a quick count. *Three men down.*

He faced front, gasped at the close enemy, their greater numbers. He crouched down, planted Jou's M-1 on a boulder, fired at a darting Japanese soldier and missed.

The soldier dove into the grass. Yuen gripped the rifle hard. A dark green cap popped up to the left. Yuen yanked the rifle over and fired two quick shots. *Damn! Nothing. Calm down!* He tried to slow his breathing. Flashes of fire from the grass. No targets. A comrade yelped next to him, on the right, falling over.

Yuen jerked the rifle right, left, scanning, frustrated. Movement in the corner of his eye, gone before he could react. Then, the soldier from before rising up right in front of him, beginning to run. Yuen took dead aim at the man's chest, leaned forward, lifted the rifle a little to get a clear shot, and squeezed the trigger.

A sudden punch in Yuen's left shoulder. He dropped Jou's rifle, his hand going to the wound. He tried to get up but another punch hit his right thigh. He felt the slug pass through to the other side. Unable to prevent it, he toppled forward into the grass.

He blinked hard and brought the mud into focus. He stared at the blades of grass, dazed. His left ear, planted in the mud, heard the vibrations of stomping feet, the echo of gunfire. The stabbing shoulder pain was intense, worse than the thigh, and it brought him back to the present. Sounds through his right ear grew louder: shots cracking, screams.

Get up. Get up!

Yuen willed himself to move. He reached for the strap of his PPS-43 automatic and slung it over his neck with his right arm. He tried to push up, but a bolt of pain lanced through his shoulder. He dropped down again.

Then hands were tugging at him, rolling him over.

David.

"We've gotta go!" David shouted.

Yuen gritted his teeth. "Leave me."

He saw David's eyes dart up, heard Bao's voice off to the left. "Go! Go! Get him out of here!"

David hoisted Yuen, tried to bring the left arm over his neck. Yuen howled. Switching to the other arm, David began to drag Yuen toward the trees, but he was dead weight.

David stopped. He knelt down and let Yuen fall over his shoulder. Grunting, he then stood, lifting Yuen with a fireman carry, and drove forward, forcing his eyes to see only the tree line thirty yards away.

Twenty yards.

Ten.

Yuen grimaced as David crossed the tree line and went up a short rise, ground drier here. David sat him down quickly and looked back.

Only four Chinese remained. They were outnumbered two to one—the attackers almost on top of them. Now fighting hand to hand. Men wrestling and tumbling to the ground.

Two Chinese were bayoneted.

Another was shot at close range.

One left standing, a big man—Bao! He'd just killed a Japanese soldier with his knife and was now wrestling with another, smashing the man's head against a boulder.

Three soldiers raised their rifles. Bao roared—his only weapon the knife—and charged. The bullets thumped into his chest. He staggered, still driving forward like an enraged animal. The Japanese soldiers scurried back, one fumbled to reload, dropping his clip in the grass. Bao slowed, stumbled, and dropped to his knees, head down, gasping for air.

One soldier lunged forward and bayoneted him in the chest.

David rolled back behind a tree trunk, breathing hard, bracing himself for what would come next. Pine needles on the tree's lower branches brushed the top of his head. He peeked around again.

Six Japanese left, shouting, pointing at him.

"Go on! Get out of here!" Yuen stammered. He slumped against the tree at David's feet.

David shook his head. He reached down and took Yuen's PPS-43 from around his neck. The stock was bent at an angle. He extended it fully and darted to his left, behind another tree, away from Yuen. Bullets whizzed by, peppering the ground. He turned, pressed close against the tree, and opened fire—hitting two soldiers.

Then: *click.*

Click.

What the hell? David lifted the rifle. The magazine was empty after only half a dozen rounds. Disgusted, he threw it aside.

Four more Japs, he counted, twenty yards away. He saw one kneel, rifle raised. David dropped behind the tree as the bullet struck bark and sent it flying like shrapnel. He drew his Colt .45, right hand shaking, sweaty-slick against the checkered grip. He pulled his dagger from its sheath with his left hand. Then he held his breath, knowing his aim was worthless at anything but point-blank range.

A quick glance showed the enemy heading straight at him, not spreading out to surround him. When he dared not wait any longer and imagined them only a few feet away, he spun and fired at the closest body.

He aimed for the soldier's chest but hit the man low in the gut. Close behind, he shot another in the shoulder, barely grazing him—but the man yowled and fell over.

A third charged with a bayoneted Arisaka. David jumped to the side to dodge the thrust, but he stumbled and fell on his back. The attacker lunged again, thrusting his bayonet into the ground inches from David's hip.

David shot him in the face.

Before David could think, he saw a blur to his right and raised his arm in defense.

A terrible pain seared his forearm as the last soldier's bayonet sliced deeply.

David dropped his pistol.

The soldier was on him, knife drawn. He wore round spectacles. Sweat dripped on the inside surface of his lenses, pooling there, magnifying his eyes.

David rolled to his left, just dodging a knife thrust near his right ear. With a hard roll back to the right, he plunged his blade, left-handed, into the man's torso.

He felt the tip hit the thin man's spine.

The soldier's body went rigid. He screamed, anguished, animal-like. David jabbed his blade in again and again. Then he pulled out and pushed the body away.

The dying man's face looked small, his glasses fallen off.

David got up and stumbled to Yuen.

The wounded Japs—he saw them now, the ones he'd shot, crawling ineffectually. He helped Yuen to his feet and they started to climb the hillside. Only then did David begin to hear the cries, the horrible howls of the eviscerated soldier.

They drove up and on, not looking back, and the sounds grew farther and farther away.

SOVIET PPS-43 "BURP GUN"

Family gun stories do not always have a convenient beginning, middle and end. Rather they seem to find their way into a conversation that begins at one point and ends up in another. Slowly, round the bend we come to the family gun, a relic, a marker of time gone by, a legend that won't die.

—The Editors

Bubba's Gun

Jonathan Huntress

My grandfather's name was Frederick but we called him Bubba. I remember him sitting quietly in his chair in the living room of their home on Bowers Street, second house to the end, smoking a pipe. My father took me and my sister Deborah to Maine in 1949. We drove there in a black 1939 Chevrolet sedan. It took five days to get there from Iowa. My mother stayed home with my new baby sister. I was five years old.

My grandfather was a plumber but his real avocation was hunting and fishing. He trapped lobsters by stretching and tying a piece of netting across a steel wagon tire, the metal rim off a wooden-spoked wagon wheel. He tied a dead fish and a brick to the middle of the net and carefully lowered it from his dory. He would have three or four of these, each with a rope attached to a wooden float. Then he would row back to the first float and slowly pull it up. There would usually be one or two lobsters on each wheel. This was around the turn of the last century when there were a lot more lobsters.

My father took his father and me and my sister to a nearby beach because we needed clams for lunch. The beach was very muddy and we would sink a few inches into the mud with every step. It was icky and I didn't like it. It was low tide, of course. You only dig for clams at low tide. Remember the expression, "Happy as a clam."? A few words got dropped from the whole expression which is, "Happy as a clam at high tide" when they are safe from the diggers like us.

My sister had no problem with the mud and waded out ten or twenty yards into the ocean. She was up to her knees and called, "Look daddy!" and held up a big horseshoe crab by its long tail. She put it back in the water after she was congratulated. My father and Bubba dug for clams and ended up with buckets full. It looked to me like hundreds. We took them home and then my father and I had to go to the store for something. When we got back I walked into the dining room and there was Bubba at the head of the table with a large pile of clam shells in front of him. "Ate all the clams!" he said, and I believed him. But when I went into the kitchen I saw Aynie, my grandmother, with a much larger pile of clams that had just been steamed on the wood stove. In 1949 she still had a wood stove that she had to fire up every morning.

I remember I was five years old and had learned how to make my own cocoa. I took a teaspoon of Hershey's powdered cocoa and two teaspoons of sugar and boiled it in a quarter cup of water then added ¾ cup of milk. I asked Aynie for a measuring cup and she gave me a regular cup. It turned out she didn't have a measuring cup or measuring spoons. I thought it was so strange and I had to guess at the amounts, but it turned out all right, which was a big surprise to me. Back then I thought you had to do everything just they way they said or it would be a disaster.

I don't think I ate many of those clams. I probably thought they were icky too.

My father said that his father remembered every duck he ever shot. Bubba had a really big gun that would have made that statement hard to believe. It was a special duck gun. They showed it to me but I have almost no memory of it except that the hole in the barrel was big. I was told you could drop a quarter down the bore. The gun was propped against the wall down in the basement but it was too tall for me to touch and it was very heavy. My father said it was actually a small cannon that just looked like a big musket. This was a punt gun. Most of them had a rod mounted mid stock that would go into a hole in the gunnel (sidewall) of the boat or punt. My father said the gun was a matchlock but I am pretty sure he was wrong about this.

The matchlock was the first attempt to fire a musket reliably. It involved a "match" which was actually a rope soaked in potassium nitrate and sulfur that turned it into a long slow burning fuse. The match would be tied to the bottom stock of the gun and looped up over the shoulder of the gunner and then would be attached to the hammer on the gun itself, continuously sputtering and smoking. The guns were loaded through the muzzle and then some fine powder would be poured into the pan. When the trigger was pulled the pan cover would rise and the match would descend into the pan and set off the gun. You always knew where your enemy was in those days because of the huge clouds of smoke from the burning matches would always give away their positions.

Flint and steel in the flintlock musket replaced the matches fairly early and were themselves largely replaced by percussion caps by the time of the Civil War. Almost all the old muskets still in use were retrofitted to caps. I am fairly sure Bubba's gun was fired with a percussion cap.

The punt gun was a very large shotgun. Some of these guns were over ten feet long and had a two inch bore. They took over a pound of black powder and fired a full pound of shot. Bubba's gun was five or six feet long, but it was still a substantial firearm. It could take out thirty or forty ducks with a single shot. Punt guns were used at night. The hunter would silently paddle as close as he could get to a flock then pull the trigger. At the sound of the explosion the flock would fly off leaving behind the dead and wounded birds.

Even though he loved the sport, Bubba always hunted for food. He took my father hunting only once. They were in a duck blind before dawn and it was very cold. My father told me he was absolutely miserable. He said it was the only time he ever told his father to shut up. Bubba forgave him. My father was a mama's boy, the last son born. He was a replacement child for his much loved older sister Agrandece, who died when she was just a year old, the year before my father was born.

My grandfather was a provider. During the Depression when nobody had any money and there was little work he would hunt and fish for food and they had a garden behind the house. On cold windy winter mornings he would walk the few blocks to Willard Beach and as the sun came up, carefully scan the sand. The wind blew the sand across the surface of the beach and when it uncovered a lost summer coin it would blow the sand out from around, leaving each coin on a little pillar of sand easy to see. One day he collected almost five dollars, a fortune during those hard times.

My father's older brother, Roderick, inherited the gun and gave it to his son, Roddy who died in March of 2015. I managed to track down his daughter who told me that her mother still has the gun, packed away in a crate in Chattanooga, Tennessee.

PUNT WITH PUNT GUN

The M-1

Peter Lauritzen

The barrel was sticking out of an old paper bag in the basement of a friend's house. We were down there poking around; I carried the bag into the light.

"It's an M-1!" I cried, recognizing the unique muzzle of the World War II icon. Or, at least part of an M-1, what's called the barreled action; the stock and trigger mechanism were missing.

"Oh, that. You can have it if you want. That was here when we moved in," said Jim, within an astounding lack of interest. I should probably note here that this was 1961—the War had been over for 16 years, but it was still very much a part of our lives, at least mine. Still is. Also, though I was only 11, I was a bit of a gun nut. I took my find home and ordered all the missing things from a gun parts warehouse.

Now, I could talk about putting the M-1 together, and ordering bandoliers of 30/06 armor-piercing (!) ammunition through the mail. I could speak of the kick of slamming an eight-round clip home, and the *sprang* the clip made when it shot up into the air, announcing to the shooter and his enemies that the gun was empty. I could recall nighttime shooting of rats at the dump with a flashlight taped to the barrel, when my cousins and I lost a generous portion of our hearing. But that's not what I wanted to talk about.

When the parts arrived, I started to assemble the gun, but I couldn't quite pull it off. I needed the help of a professional, a veteran, the salesman at the sporting goods store who had helped me figure out what parts to order in the first place. I picked up the apparently complete M-1 and walked to the bus stop.

In those days a bus ride for an adult cost 25 cents, for those under sixteen, 12 cents. I handed the driver a quarter and instead of giving me change, he tossed the coin into the hopper. I was outraged.

"Hey! I'm eleven! Where's my change?"

The driver took a long look at me through slitted eyes.

"I figure anyone getting on my bus with an M-1 should pay full fare." Another veteran. I argued my case and got my change. As I took my seat, everyone else on the bus moved away from me, to the back. Strange.

M-1 GARAND

Vagina

Bob Arnold

That was the word
Scribbled on a scrap
Of paper and given to
Me on the playground by
Albert LaFlamme, two years
Older and much taller but
We were the best of friends.
I honestly thought the word
Spelt "Virginia" and took it
To one of my teachers to see
If it was spelled right and so
Later in the week my parents
Were called into the school.
Naturally I forget what happened.

Around the same time Albert showed
Us all how strong he was by
Lifting up Junior Zabeck and
Holding him by his legs upside
Down over the cement bridge in
The center of town and Junior
Was looking high and wild at the
Hoosic River. Albert shook out
All the pocket change and a black
Comb Junior had in his pants then
Brought him back up. He'd peed all

Bob Arnold

Over himself and stood there crying
Like only fat boys can. I liked
Junior, he was my friend, but if
I said anything Albert would have
Me off the ground next. It seemed
Like an eternity but the friendship
Lasted only a few months. In that
Time Albert beat on another of my
Pals, Jon Langlois. Jon was poor

And lived in a brick tenement.
One day Jon said something
Albert didn't like so Albert ripped
The front of Jon's shirt popping off
All the different size old buttons.
Jon was a redhead and cried red.

Albert stood a good two feet over all of us.
How he fit into the casket he slept
In up in his bedroom I could never
Figure out. When he was out of the
Room during one of my visits I quickly
Lay down in the casket to try it out
For size. It was comfortable but creepy.

When Albert came bounding back up the
Stairs to his room I was smartly away
From the casket but he eyed it and me
As if he sensed something fishy then
Suggested why didn't I lie down inside

Vagina

And see what it was like. I still felt the
Cushioned liner on my fingers, the strange
Smell and declined by saying it was his
Bed and respectfully should be honored
That way. Albert liked to be king. It was
A survival instinct to make him feel like
A king. I told him he was an asshole an
Hour later though when he shot me in
The face with a bb gun. Out in his yard
Horsing around, both with loaded rifles.
I brought my head around a tree at the
Wrong time and caught the bb in the mouth
Tasting blood. Albert laughed and laughed.

I could have killed him but threw the rifle
Down on the ground and walked home fuming,
Crying eventually like all my friends...
Jon and his lost buttons; Junior and his
Flown away money and comb. I'd see Albert
Less after that, in fact it seemed like he
Disappeared from all our childhoods as if a
Bad dream. But before that happened, when
Visiting after the bb incident, somehow
Albert got me back up into his bedroom.

The casket was now passe, the lid was on.
He had no interest in shooting rifles.
There was a large mirror on his wall.
Behind the mirror Albert had roughed
Out a hole into the next apartment. In the

Apartment lived a pretty young woman who
Worked in a bank in town. She walked to
Work. Albert had her time table down like
A science. He told me every night he watched
Her undress through the hole in the wall –
Her dress, her stockings, her panties
Her tits and her vagina is how Albert
Described it. I told him I didn't believe it.

I thought he'd smack me but instead he
Rushed down the stairs and before I knew
It came these delicate taps on the other
Side of the wall, right near the peep hole.
Albert's parents were poor but they owned
The building with four apartments. It would
Be easy for a snake like Albert to get the
Keys and own the place. A louder tap came
From the wall. I approached my first peep
Hole in life and took a look and saw nothing
Until Albert moved his eye away and there he
Was sneering and giving a wave before doing
Jumping jacks on the young woman's bed.

Son of a Gun

On the Road to Israel

Alice Carney

When I was 21 years old I hitchhiked with my friend Mary from Munich, Germany to work on a kibbutz in Israel. This was 1965, decades before the Internet and cell phones. We had little knowledge of the countries we planned to travel through—Germany to Austria to Italy to Greece to Turkey to Syria to Israel—and little money. We were trusting, very naive. We had many adventures. This is a short revisit of part of the diary I kept on the journey, the days after we were kicked out of Syria and ended up in the far southern Turkish seaport town of Iskenderun.

April 7, 1965

I just fell down a rabbit hole and landed in a place where the cultural mores are upside-down from what I have known. When I was a teenager, my father, a retired Army officer, said to me, "You are book smart, but son of a gun, sometimes you just don't think. You need to be more careful." Meaning, be careful when you flirt, watch yourself when you walk down the street alone, both of which I found "old-fashioned" attitudes and confining. When I turned twenty-one I still thought male attention was a badge of honor, that I could be friendly, and innocent, and admired all at the same time. In southwestern Turkey I learned that that combination of naïveté, adventure-seeking, ignorance, and entitlement could bring disaster, could be the spark that sends a bullet ricocheting through a room full of people.

***

March 31, 1965 Iskenderun, Turkey

After traveling the length of Turkey, my hitchhiking partner Mary and I were turned back from the Syrian border. This was the time of Ramadan and Turkish pilgrims, mostly men, were making the journey to Mecca. Late at night we joined hundreds of them as they crossed the three miles from Reyhanlı in Turkey to the small Syrian border post of Cilvegözü. The Syrian guards were tired and cranky. We increased their crankiness by telling them that we were traveling through Syria to go work on a kibbutz in Israel.

"Israel!" screamed the uniformed border guard, his brass badges, his military issue revolver flashing in its leather holster on his waist, "You are friends with Israel?!!" Hours of angry interrogation, emptying and examining of each item in our backpacks, of guards tweaking our hair, making offers whose words we could not understand, but whose intent we could. *Whomp!* Large black inked Arabic stamps on our passports.

"See, this says you are friends with Israel. You are never welcome in Syria!" and he sent us, under armed guard, to stand in the middle of the dark road until a west bound truck came along and gave us a midnight ride back to Turkey.

After an hour of bouncing in the cold, open back of the truck, we stopped in the middle of Iskenderun, here on the coast of the Mediterranean. The driver spoke only Turkish and Arabic. We spoke only English and smatterings of German. He was not unkind, but we could tell that he had no idea what to do with us. Iskenderun was a small town in those days, no youth hostels, no hotels open. There were few lights. A cold breeze blew down from the mountains behind us, a damp open sewer smell came from a trench in the stones of the street where we stood.

Just as we were feeling truly forlorn, up walked an Iskenderun policeman. Because the spring was still cold, he wore the winter uniform, an over-sized heavy brown wool jacket with huge shoulder pads and sleeves that allowed only his finger tips to show. His hat, similar to a military officer's hat, too big for him, sat below his eyebrows; only his eyes and mustache peeked out. He nodded seriously after the driver explained our plight, and signaled for us to follow him down the empty street. We entered a gateway, crossed a patio, and were in the police station.

The main room was like an old-fashioned police station from the Old West: a wood-burning pot-bellied stove in the corner, benches along the wall, desks and piles of old papers and books, an uncovered electric light bulb dangling from the ceiling. A large portrait of Ataturk on the paint-peeled wall. Four uniformed policemen. To our relief, the young handsome one, Metin, spoke pretty good English. When they heard our story, the policemen laughed, told us we were welcome in Turkey, brought us tea, and had us stretch our sleeping bags around the stove for the night.

The floor was hard and cold, the stove smoked, but we were glad to have a place to be out of the dark. Just before sunrise, one of the policemen put his jacket across my back.

In the morning, over tea and yogurt, we talked with Metin about how to get to Israel. Ships often came into the port, then headed back to Haifa, so we decided to wait a day or two, then sail off to Israel. Metin found us this hotel, and after dropping our backpacks in our room, we set off exploring Iskenderun. By the middle of the afternoon, we were sitting on the rocks by the port, talking how long it would take for a boat to come, one day, two days? Behind us was a growing crowd of young boys and men, just standing, watching us. When we walked away, to escape from them, they followed, did not leave until we turned into the entrance to the police station.

In addition to the problems at the Syrian border, this is the time of another conflict between Turkey and Greece over the island Cyprus, out there in the Mediterranean, half way between us and Israel. Iskenderun is the main port of entry and departure for Turkish troops, so there is an abundant supply of uneducated, unoccupied men on the street, many of whom come from isolated villages, are unaccustomed to women wandering by themselves. The police decided that it was not safe for us to walk alone through the city and we are now under the custody of Metin, whom, thankfully, we can trust—and with strict orders to talk to no one, to keep our room locked, and not to go out alone—a rather novel situation for the two of us. Our main communication today has been with two six year old boys who carefully bring us our tea.

4 pm

Twenty-five young soldiers are now billeted on the floor outside our room so I am not sure how we are any safer in the hotel than out. We stuff our keyhole with Kleenex to keep them from peeking in at us.

There is a dingy septic sewer smell of the only "toilette" on our floor. We share this with the soldiers, so carefully time when we go in and out. The toilet is in a small dark room, it is a cement square with footholds on each side of the hole over which one squats. It smells of open sewer. Funk. There is a water tap in the corner for washing. I keep my shoes on when I am in there. This morning, when I was leaving that room, a young Turkish recruit was standing outside the door, waving a lacy woman's nightgown at me. I rushed past him, locked the door of our room, stuffed the Kleenex back in the keyhole, more indignant than scared.

Our room is on the third floor and has balconies on two sides. Mary and I spend a lot of time out on the balcony, looking down the market, a dirt road crowded on both sides with stone buildings, striped awnings, food stands piled with oranges, pomegranates, pistachios, olives, tomatoes, white goat cheeses. There is the smell of the dust, horse manure, people's bodies mixing together. We can hear the vendors calling out their wares, their voices mixing with religious chants from the mosques, bells on the donkeys, and mournful flutes. Children are also vendors, selling breads that are like big round pretzels with sesame seeds, looped over a stick. I see one little girl, bone thin, with a bandana around her head, a tattered blouse with full sleeves, a lavender vest, and floppy striped pantaloons, standing alone in the dust at the end of the street, holding her breaded stick high above her head. She has dark eyes and no smile.

The colors are the blues of the eastern Mediterranean (which we can see on our right) set against white plastered buildings, flashes of dark, deep purples and greens of woman's skirts and pantaloons, soft scarves covering their heads. Few pastels to be seen anywhere. There is constant movement on the street, donkey-pulled carts and horse-drawn carriages, plus the little boys weaving in and out, delivering "chi" (tea in small clear glasses) on silver platters. The men are dressed mostly in brown or black, with soft caps and baggy pants. They sit in the dark coffee shops, drinking the small cups of Turkish coffee, talking, looking, watching. We never see women in the coffee shops.

Our abode is, apparently, a prostitutes' domain (our main guardian in the hotel is named Fatima—her hair is a brilliant bottled red, her teeth widely spaced, make-up heavy, body paunchy, age around forty, another of our own private guardian angels). We had asked Metin to find us a cheap place to live, and he did.

April 4, 1965 Iskenderun

Mary is having trouble with her metabolism, we think the pills pre-
scribed in Istanbul to activate her thyroid are actually depressing it. She
sleeps a lot. I've spent some time at the police station two blocks away,
just visiting. I sit on a bench and watch the people arguing, gesticulat-
ing, crying. I don't understand a word. This afternoon a thin, ragged
teenage boy was brought in. Two of the police started hitting him, pushing him to the floor. He moaned and yelled wild distressed sounds. He
obviously was mute, perhaps deaf. I left. I don't think I will go back.
The police staff (all male) work six hour shifts, which means that they
are never fully rested, always tired and irritable.

This is our third day here, we are still waiting for a boat to Israel.

April 5, 1965

Yesterday Fatima took us to the public Turkish baths. First real bath
in an awfully long time. We were escorted to stalls where we disrobed
and wrapped ourselves in large white towels, watched all the time by a
silent little girl who then led us into a central, steaming room filled with
fat, naked, pendulous breasted women sitting on stools, surrounded by
small children skidding around the wet tile floor on their naked bottoms.
Around the sides of the room were more stalls where we had buckets of
hot water poured over us, then several women soaped us down until we
were covered with a thick white lather; then with a rough black cloth
they scrubbed and scrubbed our skin. I remember the rolls of grey dirt
and old skin cells piling up along my arm, being rinsed off, sliding down
the drain, my embarrassment that I could have been so dirty. Our hair
was washed, scalp rubbed and rinsed, then we were moved to the next
stall, where it was done all over again. Finally we were led back into the

center of the room, to sit in the steam, skin pink and glowing, to converse in sign language with the other naked ladies.

Did we have children? No.

Were we married? No.

How old were we? 21 and 23.

No children? Sorrowful shakes of the head.

Scrutiny of Mary's body. She is taller than I, strong-boned. Positive shakes of heads. You will have good children. My boney body, skinny rump, invited barely a glance, and that probably of pity: not built for breeding.

We left the baths refreshed and clean.

I am thinking the baths are the symbol of the women's world for me, a chance finally to be comfortable after days of feeling like objects of prey in a male-dominated world. Outside that moist, steamy, safe bath house, we could not walk the streets in safety, we were objects, the looked upon, rather than people. It is funny to look back now, to see how far I have physically traveled to experience "life" and "freedom" and have ended up in a situation of more confinement and threat than I have ever known. It feels like men's eyes are guns, aimed at us, confining us.

Which is why last night will always stay in my memory, the closest that I have ever come to being shot or attacked.

This is what happened:

Metin wanted to treat us to a celebration dinner. We had been eating in our room the past three days and, we were hoping a ship would be there any day to take us away. He surprised us at the front door with a horse-drawn carriage—and a friend of his, Ahmet, whom he assured us, was a "good man," married with three children. The horse clopped us to a restaurant in a part of town we had not been in before. There was music, women in bright colors and make-up, gaiety and laughter.

Ahmet, who could not speak English and we could not speak Turkish, kept looking at Mary, a loopy smile on his face. After a dinner of kabobs, onions, eggplant, peppers, hot flat bread, yogurt, and beer, Ahmet and Metin talked, then suggested we take a taxi to a bus stop outside of Iskenderun, for Raki, an unsweetened, anise flavored alcoholic drink. Why not, we said. We are with friends, this may be our last night in Iskenderun. Let's celebrate.

We drove miles and miles up a twisting mountain road. By the time we arrived at the bus stop I felt anxious. I saw no buses, just a battered truck, a few old cars, one taxi. The bus stop sat by itself off the road, a yellowed, stone building, sparsely furnished, with flickering electric lights, people moving around in the dark outside. But we trusted Metin and Ahmet was considered trustable because he was older, a policeman, and a friend of Metin's. And we were out of the hotel room, our stomachs were full, we had had beer and the Raki was a local treat.

At first it seemed like a nice party, six of us in a private room, just off the front entry room. Another couple had appeared when we arrived and invited themselves to join us. We thought they were acquaintances of Metin's. Having another woman with us made me feel a bit better. We drank Raki, ate thousands of pistachio nuts, laughed a lot, and I relaxed. We seemed to be having a great, innocent time. Until Ahmet, whom by now I noticed had beady green eyes, began to talk loudly and wave his arms, ordering more and more Raki. At the same time Mary's metabolism started slowing down so that she couldn't stay awake. We three women were sitting on a bench along the wall, facing the door. The men were opposite us. To add to the uneasiness of the situation, I had developed an acute case of dysentery which hadn't been helped by the meal and the pistachio nuts. Every five minutes I would have to slide off the bench seat and run outside to the toilet (Oriental: ceramic square in the ground, a hole in the center, a foothold on each side, ancient scent of human waste) and Metin would follow to stand guard at the door, hand on pistol at his waist.

Soon it became evident to us that bus stops are rowdy places and we were among the more sober people there. The entrance room at the front was filling with more and more drunken, yelling men, many of whom kept running to our door and staring in. There we were, Mary falling asleep, the woman with us insisting through sign-language that she could find a bed for Mary to sleep on—*Aghhh!* And Ahmet getting drunker, more obnoxious, smiling, reaching across the table to touch Mary's hair. Metin was well behaved, though rather tipsy by this point. He kept fingering his gun, snapping and unsnapping the leather holster, each time a group of men looked in at us.

Suddenly, there were two shots from outside. Metin jumped up and ran out. Much shouting and yelling. I couldn't understand what was happening, but I could feel sweat running down my sides. This was not the adventure I had wanted. We were in a very isolated place, in a culture we did not know, with people with whom we could not communicate, surrounded by drunk men shooting guns. I looked around that barren room. Mary's eyes half-closed, chin to chest; Ahmet leering greasily; and drunks running past our door. I had a flash of realization that I had not been just naive all this time, I had been stupid.

Metin rushed back in, his pistol gleaming in his hand, and shouted to me in broken English that we were his sisters, that even if ten men and himself must be shot, no one would touch us. He and Ahmet argued loudly in Turkish.

Trapped there in the midst of what Metin called men's "hunger," the liquor, and almost everyone carrying pistols, I heard my father voice: "Son of a gun, you have gotten yourself in a big mess now! Be careful and get out of there!"

"You need to take us out of here now!" I shouted at Metin. His eyes cleared, he stood up straight, waved his pistol, and shouted, in English, "Yes, we are out of here!" We grabbed Mary, shook her awake, ignored the pleas of the other woman, who was still pointing at Mary, signing about beds, pulled Ahmet by the arm, and ran into the dark parking lot through the mumbling crowd of sweaty, alcohol-reeking men, into a taxi that Metin somehow conjured up for us, and skidded out onto the road, Metin waving his pistol and yelling out the window, "We are out of here. You will not touch my sisters!"

We descended the twisting mountain road. Ahmet pouted, Mary slept, and Metin apologized. I stared out the window at the stars over the Mediterranean, my imagination filling in the blanks of what could have happened. As we drove into the dark streets of Iskenderun, up to our shabby hotel, I could feel my heartbeats finally starting to slow down. We had been lucky, we were unscathed. I vowed to myself that I would never, ever, put myself into that risky of a situation again.

The next day a sober Metin came by. The police had found us passage to Israel. In an hour we had rolled up our sleeping bags, stuffed our one change of clothes, toothbrushes, and books into our backpacks, given Fatima a hug, stepped past four staring army recruits, and left Iskenderun.

My one regret, now, is that I never reconnected with Metin, let him know that we arrived safely in Israel, are working in the apple orchards on a kibbutz. I should have thanked him and the Iskenderun police for watching over us.

The Momaday Gun

N. Scott Momaday

Do I have Billy the Kid's gun? Billy and I think so, but of course we cannot prove it. I attach my argument, which was published in True West magazine. Billy is amused by the controversy.

Be well,

Scott

This is the story of a gun, a handgun that appears to have belonged to Billy the Kid. I have been deeply interested in the life and times of Billy the Kid for many years, and I have written widely on that subject in poetry, fact, and fiction.

I purchased the gun from my friend Will Channing of Santa Fe, with whom it had been placed for auction. Knowing of my interest in Billy the Kid, Will informed me by telephone that the gun was available. I was dubious. Immediately I asked, "Is it a .41 caliber Colt 'Thunderer?' Will answered, "Yes." And I became excited; I knew that that particular model was the Kid's weapon of choice. As I recall, I obtained the gun in or about 1983. It has been in my possession ever since.

With the gun, as an item of provenance, came a notarized statement as follows:

To whom it may concern:

> *This particular piece has been in my family, at least to my knowledge, for over 90 years. The 41 cal. Colt is believed to have been used by William H. Bonney alias Billy the Kid for whom I am named.*

This is supposedly the gun that was hidden in a juniper tree after his famous escape from Lincoln County April 28, 1881. He had given the gun to Teresa Guererro who was my great great grandmother and has been passed down to the eldest son in each generation until now.

Signed

William H. Bonney II

This original document bears the signatures of William H. Bonney II and Janice (Bolinger) Blevins, notary of the state of New Mexico, in their respective hands. It is dated August 7, 1982. Ms. Blevins, on the same document, swears and affirms that she was witness to the purchase by Bob Ward of the gun on June 9, 1976 at the Original Trading Post in Santa Fe, New Mexico. At that time she declares that she examined the identification card presented by William H Bonney II and found it to be genuine. Bob Ward was a well-known trader and owned the Original Trading Post.

I am not so naïve as to believe that "William H. Bonney II" is the real name of a real person. If it were, he would surely be visible, even conspicuous on account of his name. Here is, one is bound to conclude, an imposture, a ruse concocted perhaps to facilitate the sale of the gun. Be that as it may, the fact is that someone, a real person, signed that name to a bill of sale before a notary public in 1982. Who was that man?

From the time of Billy the Kid's escape from the Lincoln County Court House on April 28, 1881 to the time of his death on July 14, 1881, almost nothing is known of him. Between Lincoln and Fort Sumner, NM, in the last 81 days of his life, he became a legend and a virtual ghost. And in this period the Momaday gun takes on a mantle of special importance. In this obscure interval, was it in the hands of Billy the Kid?

In a letter dated February 16, 2012, I received a letter from Beverly Jean Haynes, Historian at the Colt Manufacturing Company, Hartford, CT authenticating the Momaday gun. The .41/c Colt double action revolver of 1877 bears the serial number 26048. It has a barrel length of 2 ½ inches and is finished in nickel with rubber stocks. It was shipped to N. Curry and Brothers of San Francisco, CA on May 11, 1881. There were 10 guns of the same type in the shipment. It is significant that the gun was shipped to San Francisco instead of a distribution center in the East. Ordinarily, guns going to the West were sent to St. Louis, MO. Remarkably, Billy the Kid and the gun were both in New Mexico Territory at the same time. We do not know to whom the gun was sent or carried from San Francisco, but we know that it ended up in New Mexico. There was a considerable commerce in handguns in El Paso, Las Cruces, Roswell, Albuquerque, Santa Fe, Las Vegas, Fort Sumner, and other settlements.

Now we come again to the William H. Bonney II document and the name Guererro. Guererro is a common name of Spanish origin in New Mexico, and it is entirely possible that the Kid knew one or more persons of that name. Moreover we know that the Kid spoke Spanish fluently and that the Spanish speaking people of his time and place held him fast in their affection and that they protected him from those who were hunting him down.

I have not yet been able to identify Teresa Guererro. Was she too a fiction, or was she perhaps a great great grandparent of the man sin nombre, as he claims she was. I can easily imagine that she was one of the numerous senoritas who shared a romantic bond with Billy the Kid. Did she or her family offer succor to him? And in affection and/or gratitude did he give her the gun? It would have been a grand gesture— the young, dashing, famous outlaw gifting her with the valuable hardware, the very tool of his trade. Billy could well afford to be generous.

He is known to have left Lincoln with several guns from the Court House armory, though not this one. The Momaday gun, given the information provided by the Colt Manufacturing Company, must have been acquired closer to the time of his death. He surely jettisoned one or more guns in order to travel with less of a burden.

From the middle of May to the time of his death, there is a critical window of opportunity. It is likely that Billy purchased guns in his lifetime. We know that he traded for one or more. In those final days he might have bought, stolen, or traded for the gun, this gun. Clifford R. Caldwell, in his book, Guns of the Lincoln County War, reports, "Legend has it that a man named Cherokee Davis, who worked as a cook for John Chisum, was given a new .41 Caliber Thunderer by Chisum on 4 July 1881. When Billy rode into Chisum's cow camp along the Pecos he saw Davis's Thunderer and took an immediate liking to it. Billy proposed a …trade with Davis…" This was only 10 days before Billy's death, but for the sake of possibility, Caldwell's statement ought to be taken into account. Was the Momaday gun sent by N. Curry and Brothers of San Francisco to John Chisum?

The William H. Bonney II statement and the Colt Manufacturing Company letter of authenticity provide convincing information. And again, the fact that Billy and the gun were in the same place at the same time, together with the fact that the 1877 .41 caliber Colt Thunderer was Billy's favorite weapon, notably support the argument that the Momaday gun belonged to Billy the Kid. The preponderance of all available evidence is positive.

Bob Ward is deceased. William H. Bonney II and Janice Bolinger Blevins have vanished and are presumed dead. Teresa Guererro is lost somewhere in the mists of history. Yet each of these souls has affirmed in one way or another that the Momaday gun was once in the possession of Billy the Kid.

I am all but convinced. I find the evidence, in its totality, compelling.

Finally, let me set forth what to me is the most important and indisputable consideration of all. The Momaday gun is a real and essential artifact of the Wild West, that dimension of history and lore that has so largely shaped the American imagination. Indeed there is no Wild West without Billy the Kid, as there is none without this gun, whatever its history. When you look at the Momaday gun, when you hold it in your hand as Billy the Kid seems so likely to have done, you enter into a sphere of instinct that truly defines the American experience. Here is a whole and true story in itself, and the story will forever involve Billy the Kid and his gun. The gun belongs to Billy, and Billy belongs to us.

N. Scott Momaday 2012

P.S. In a dream Billy the Kid comes to me, and we confer:

–Well, Scott, I see you've got my gun.

–How do I know it's yours?

–Take my word for it. Have I ever lied to you?

–They say no one can prove that it's yours.

–Well, sure as shootin', no one can prove that it ain't.

–I like the odds, Billy.

–You bet, amigo.

COLT .41 THUNDERER REVOLVER

Divine Providence

Rebecca Godfrey-Poe

"You want me to go to Providence with you?!"

Rosalind nearly hung up the phone. "Henry, you have such nerve!"

"Look, we need this project. We are obligated by duty . . ."

"Duty?"

"Uh, yeah, to one another . . . you know as well as I do, Roz, how much we need the money. Well, I need the money. Look, this is our chance to become known and to secure those tenure-track jobs. . . . If you could put aside your petty differences . . ."

"Petty differences?" And, with that, Rosalind hung up the phone.

"Providence," she said to herself. "We had never made it to Providence during our marriage, so why should I go with him now?"

Rosalind and Henry met the summer of 2003 at Penn State. He was a graduate student—an English major—studying with the help from the Poe Studies Association. Henry was a terrible student, but his distant family connection to Poe allowed him to keep his scholarship. Miss Rosalind Riley-Reed was giving a presentation, along with her mentor, the acclaimed Poe scholar, Dr. Edmund Stokes. Her parents had been furious she had selected the state school, first for her bachelor's degree and now for her graduate degree. Her father was a Princeton man, a linguist, now teaching at Tulane. He didn't have to work—he was an old-liner, whose family had made their money years before in the merchant business. Still, he enjoyed teaching and enjoyed hearing himself talk (in many languages). Her mother had graduated from Harvard, as had all of her family before her. She passed her days attending Uptown social circle events, gardening at their St. Charles Avenue home, and finding new ways to spend the family money. Rosalind's parents could

131

not understand their daughter's strange obsession with Edgar Allan Poe and certainly could not understand why she would take a scholarship to Louisiana State. A daughter of their means did not require a scholarship—it was embarrassing. For the most part, however, Rosalind got along well with her family and could recall having had but two fights with her parents—first, when she told them she was heading to Baton Rouge to make her own way in this world and the day she had announced her elopement with Henry.

Henry Poe: Henry had no middle name. His parents thought middle names were pretentious. They disliked formal names, as well. Henry's sister was named Katie. Simply Katie—not Katherine. Mr. Poe questioned the value in giving someone a formal name, especially as the person would be called by a nickname anyway. They had no problem with nicknames.

The Poes lived halfway between Baltimore, Maryland and Harper's Ferry, West Virginia in a small, rural community. The unmarried Katie or Katie-Did, as her brothers called her, was the middle child. Katie still resided at home and taught third grade at the local school. Jack was the baby brother, and he did his best to shun a formal education. Still, of the two siblings, Henry was closer to his brother. Henry had always been an excellent student.

The family was thrilled when he had won the scholarship to Penn State, but this was the first time Henry had been away from home, and he found himself uncomfortable, being so terribly far away from family. He suffered tremendously from homesickness and started drinking to relieve his anxiety. Henry was brilliant, but his grades suffered. That would change when he met his "Roz."

Henry had restlessly settled into his seat after a short coffee break. The last presenter was soon to set up, and he kept watching his watch, wishing he could make time pass a bit faster. He hated these events but knew, as the selected scholar for the Poe Studies Association, he had to be there. He had given his presentation earlier that morning, and it was the best-received presentation. It was.

The afternoon had featured some very dull speakers, and Henry imagined this last one would be the same. He had briefly met the woman. She was pretty but not his type. She was petite and looked much younger than her age, and, although she was from the South, she did not have the same lovely, lilting Tidewater accent shared by his mother and sister. In fact, she had a patrician quality to her in speech and dress, and Henry found both very off-putting. When she started her presentation however, Henry was fixated by her witty introduction, and found her ability to weave research, pop culture, and a sense of humor into such solid scholarship incredible. For such a small woman, she commanded the room. He thought to himself, "Pretty hair."

They would not see one another for four years. They met again at another Poe Studies Association Conference. This time, Rosalind was the featured speaker. Henry hadn't been back to these conferences—he had been busy teaching as an adjunct and applying to doctoral programs; however, when he noticed the conference program announcement, he decided to see if Miss Riley-Reed was still as pretty. He knew she would still be smart. Although not sanctioned by her parents, the Poe marriage, which took place only three months later, was a successful one, at least for the first three years. They had compromised and moved to Baltimore and took what to most would be an unbearably small studio. The newlyweds didn't mind the close quarters, and they could spend their free time walking along the harbor and talking. Roz, as Henry called her, liked being in a city and liked being near the water. Henry liked not being too far from his parents and sister. Brother Jack had followed his heart—and a beautiful redhead—to Kentucky right after his high school graduation.

The Poes' daughter had been born just eleven months after their marriage. Roz insisted on calling her Seraphina Lee, naming her after her paternal grandmother and her maternal grandfather. It was a fine choice according to Mr. Reed, and he would give a lengthy dissertation on the linguistic attributes of the child's first name to anyone who would listen (or be forced to listen). Henry's parents were not so sure about the choice and decided to call the baby Sera, pronounced Sara. Upon hearing this, Mr. Reed quipped, "Qué será, será!"

Rosalind and Henry both were in doctoral programs and employed by the university as teaching assistants, and, although money and time were tight, theirs was a happy home. That would change on Christmas Eve, just three days shy of Sera's third birthday. Rosalind had planned to spend the holidays in New Orleans.

The Reed house, located in the central part of the Audubon Place neighborhood, was always gorgeous, but even more so at Christmas with all of the decorations. There was a Christmas tree in each room and each had a theme. The jazz and the bourbon flowed. Roz loved to ride the wreath-decorated trolley into the French Quarter to enjoy the traditional *réveillon* and the bonfire on the levee, to help Papa Noel find his way.

Henry found himself very uncomfortable at the Riley-Reed celebrations. For one thing, he disliked the formality of the holidays. He felt out of place with the lavish meals and hated the idea of being in a suit for the entire length of the stay, and now they had a rambunctious toddler to add to the stress. He also hated to be around the temptations of alcohol. Although any one of those explanations would have sufficed for Roz, she knew Henry wanted to spend Christmas with his brother in Somerset, Kentucky, and so that is why she made the suggestion.

Jack's beloved wife had been killed in an automobile accident on her way home from her nightshift job at the 7-Eleven, leaving Jack to raise their young children, Annie, who was the same age as Sera, and Henry, the six-year-old named after his uncle.

Although they were not expected until Christmas morning, Henry drove the nine hours straight to arrive on Christmas Eve.

Far from being well off, Jack had a built a delightful cabin in the woods for his family. When they pulled up, the Poes noticed the half-strewn lights on the front of the cabin. Jack came around from the back of the property with a hunting rifle in his hand.

"That's some way to greet your brother! Now, look, I bought you a better present this year!" Henry yelled.

"I wasn't expecting you until morning, Henry."

Pointing to the side of the property, Henry explained the gun: "Damn bobcat is getting a little too close for comfort. He is hunting the deer, but I can't have him this close to the house and kids . . . My God, is that you, Roz? Gorgeous as ever! Give the handsome Poe brother a kiss, will you? Where is Sera? Where's my little Pound Cake, my little Sera Lee?

"Oh, goodness, don't call her that name, Jack. Seraphina is asleep in the car. Henry insisted on driving all day and night."

***

"The kids are already asleep. Annie sleeps in my room now—she has had nightmares ever since Shelly died. Put my little Pound Cake in Annie's room next to Henry's. Yes, I washed the sheets," Jack said with a laugh.

Roz carried the sound-asleep Sera in to bed. Jack and Henry walked into the living room. Jack put the rifle down and motioned to Henry. "Come give your brother a hug, you old lug. I'll hug up that pretty wife of yours if you don't."

When Roz came back, the three headed back outside. "Help me get the lights up, if you don't mind. Damn cat got me distracted, and I want to have these up. I know, it's not as pretty as New Orleans, Roz, but we do the best we can around here."

They laughed and reminisced and had just finished stringing the lights. Henry and Roz stood there waiting for Jack to give the lights a test when they heard the sound of a gunshot, followed by the sounds of a crying child.

In an instant, all of their lives had changed. Seraphina Lee Poe had died from a single shot to the head, killed instantly and accidentally by her cousin who had been proudly showing off his father's rifle.

The accident certainly strained the relationship of the two close brothers, but it would destroy the Poe marriage, mostly because Henry couldn't put the accident behind him. He found it impossible to discuss, feeling such remorse and guilt, not only for himself and his wife but also for what it did to his brother. Jack committed suicide just one month later, using the very same rifle.

Henry had suggested they take in the two children, but that and Henry's constant drinking proved too much for Rosalind. She left Henry and moved back to New Orleans. Henry moved back with his parents, sister, niece and nephew but returned back after three months to the apartment he had shared with Roz in Baltimore. His parents became too critical of his evenings out and his spending. Roz had been sending Henry monthly checks, thinking it would help him, but it only made him feel like more of a failure.

They had been separated for nearly three years when Henry saw the publication notice for a new book on Poe. It was a historical fiction piece on Poe's relationship with Fanny Sargent Osgood. He ordered it on Amazon and had it read the day it arrived. He called Roz at midnight:

"Should I send it to you? I can send it out Priority tomorrow. It's a delightful read."

"It's speculation, Henry. It's fabrication. You know I hate that stuff."

Roz had always been the logical one, the "Great Purveyor of Truths," as Henry liked to tease. Henry preferred the gray areas, half-truths, rumors, and innuendos, and, if it were a truth that he'd rather not hear or think about, he could choose to ignore it.

"Well, okay, why don't you investigate the truth, Roz? Let's prove whether or not theirs was a romantic relationship. Let's prove Fanny Fay was or was not—I say was—Poe's daughter. Remember what we read on that Poe fan page: "Truth long lies hidden but time's long-delayed opportunity at length comes to light–the things that have long been concealed. Truth is the daughter of time." Henry didn't really know what he was saying, but he didn't want Roz to hang up. She hung up.

Henry called her every day for nearly two weeks. During this time, he had hatched a scheme to go to Providence to do research into the life of Frances "Fanny" Sargent Osgood. He thought it might turn into something. Maybe, just maybe, it would turn their lives around.

He made a last-ditch effort: "Fine, Roz, our marriage is over, oh but wait, Ms. Technicality, it isn't officially over. You never had it annulled. Besides, even if it were over, we could still collaborate. Even if we don't get a publishable article out of it, we might use it as fodder for a book."

"Good God, Henry, you are delusional. We cannot get along, so how could we possibly collaborate? And, now, let me get this straight, we might not have enough material for a journal article, but a book is in the realm of possibility? Sober up, Henry."

The last comment stung. He knew she was right about that part, but he knew he was right about the need to investigate the Poe-Osgood relationship. He couldn't explain why to her or to himself—he just felt it.

It would take two more weeks of daily calls to convince Roz to go to Providence with him.

Providence. Of all places—Providence! Roz had assumed her parents would pay for their honeymoon. They had paid for her sister's, and Roz didn't want some expensive Baltic Sea cruise. She wanted to go to Providence. Although she had been to Maine, New York, and Boston and had spent many childhood summers on Martha's Vineyard, she had never made it to Rhode Island. Henry had written his graduate thesis on the relationship between Mrs. Sarah Helen Whitman and Poe, but he had never been to Providence, as much as he wanted to study the Whitman-Poe courtship there. Roz was sorely disappointed that her parents had decided that no Catholic wedding also meant no gift of a honeymoon. Instead, and much to Henry's dismay, they received a Reed family heirloom—an English 18th century sterling silver tea service. Henry was not impressed.

"An afternoon tea is a lovely ritual, Henry."

"You should have figured out by the elopement that I hate rituals, Roz."

***

He would be unsuccessful in his multiple requests to have Roz sell the silver. Each year, he would promise to take Roz to Providence for their anniversary, but always something took the money he had saved . . .the down-payment for the new apartment . . . a used car when their inherited BMW finally stopped running . . . a child's funeral.

It was on a Sunday, two weeks after Henry first called about Providence that Roz accepted the invitation. "It's conditional, Henry, like your love."

"That's really not necessary, Roz, but it seems to indicate you have emotions after all! Shall I alert the newspapers? What will your mother think about this, Roz?"

"Henry, you are not funny. Look, I will go with you if you agree to an annulment when we return."

"Oh, I get it. Full circle. You have to make everything complete."

After a dreadful amount of silence, Roz quietly said she would make the arrangements.

"Of course you will, of course you will. Wait. Don't hang up. Roz?"

"Yes."

"You get the airfare, but let me get the housing. Let's start with two weeks."

"Two weeks. If after two weeks we do not have anything good with which to work, we'll part ways."

"Fine. Two weeks."

"Shit. How am I going to pay for two weeks in Providence?" Henry sat and thought and looked at the laptop he recently bought on Craigslist.

"Craigslist! That's it! Hell, it's a college town. There is sure to be a sublet. Some poor fellow has already flunked out of his first semester, some dumb sod like me." Henry muttered to himself.

Henry did find a sublet and on Benefit Street.

"Benefit Street? You found a house on Benefit Street? Have you gone mad? Next thing you know, we'll spend the next two weeks on Brattle Street in Cambridge. Ha!"

"Would you like to? Go to Cambridge, I mean. Fanny is buried at Mt Auburn."

"Henry. I am not even going to get into such a ridiculous conversation. I'll call you again with the flight information."

They met three weeks later at the Providence Airport.

"My first uneventful flight, maybe this bodes well, Henry."

Rosalind's hope would be short-lived. It was not a house on Benefit Street, but a dark and musty basement apartment in a multi-family house on Benefit Street. Henry hoped she would appreciate the location and the convenience to the Athenaeum and to Brown. She didn't.

The first night was miserable. The apartment was damp and dusty and cold. "Of course I could buy a space heater, Henry, but I think it serves us well to suffer. Then, we will never ever want to look back at this point."

For nearly two weeks, the two worked diligently in the special collections at Brown and at the Athenaeum, but not much came of their efforts. Henry tried to encourage Roz, noting the timing of the departure of Ms. Osgood's husband for California. He left the same year Edgar Allan Poe died.

Roz didn't react. Henry tried again.

"And isn't it odd, Roz, how Samuel Osgood has a sculpture designed and installed for Fanny's grave which he stated was inspired by The Hand that Swept the Sounding Lyre, the poem she wrote in memory of Poe!"

"Well, he also threatened to sue Elizabeth Ellet for defamation for the accusations against his wife."

"Okay, but what do you make of the fact that Fanny sent Margaret Fuller and Anne—what's her last name"

"Lynch"

"Yes, Annie Lynch. So, why would she send them to the Poe cottage to retrieve the correspondence she had with Poe. Oh, if we only had those lost letters."

"I make nothing of it, Henry. I can't make anything of it. We have no facts. Look, we need to give up. I am tired, and I don't find this interesting anymore. I don't find myself interesting anymore, and I certainly do not find Providence interesting anymore."

"I haven't given up, Roz. Hey, there is a Water Fire performance tonight. Let's go and enjoy the evening. I know I should have asked you, but I picked up a couple of masks for us. The theme is a carnivale, but you can leave it to Henry to bring the magic!"

"We are not on vacation. I think you need to put away the mask, Henry, and realize . . ." Roz's voice trailed off.

"I realize a lot more than you realize." Henry grabbed his mask. Roz, I am going to dinner, and I am going to the performance tonight."

Roz told herself she would write, but she found herself unable to work, and she found herself nearly in tears. She didn't know the reason exactly, except she knew the reason was Henry. She put on her mask and went to find him.

The crowd was much larger than she expected. After quite a bit of searching, she found a spot by the river and sat down, peering out at the water and the reflections. Henry was right—this was special. Just as she had that thought, she heard the familiar sound of Henry's laughter. He was behind her, teasing a young girl, ever the trickster. The little girl waved goodbye and walked with her mother to a vendor. Roz could tell she was pining for a light stick. The mother shook her head and started to walk off, pulling the child away. Roz watched Henry run over and purchase the stick, taking it to the delighted child. "She must be the same age Seraphina would be. Oh, and doesn't she have the same auburn hair." Roz quickly turned around, clenched her fists and jaw, and hoped Henry wouldn't see her.

Roz pretended to be asleep when Henry came in, except he fell over the futon on his way to the bathroom and landed with a thud.

"Henry, what in Hades!"

"I'm drunk, Roz. That's what they call it. Would you like to smell my breath? Come here and kiss me."

"I can smell you from here."

Henry ran over, knocking off Roz's books and notebooks, and attempted to kiss her.

"Get out. Get out. I hate this. I hate drunks."

"You hate me? You hate me? Wow, I didn't think you had this level of *intensity*, Roz. It's sexy. You should try this more often." Henry grabbed Roz's head, wrapped his fingers around her fine auburn hair, and kissed her.

Roz slapped Henry. "Get out! Get out or I will call the police."

"Fine. That's just beautiful, Roz. You're beautiful, Roz. I, I . . ." Henry tumbled into the hall and looked back.

"Get out! I haaa . . ." Roz didn't finish her sentence.

***

Henry slammed the door and made his way to the Amtrak station. Without a suitcase, without much of anything, he bought a ticket for the last train to New York. He needed to be with family.

He arrived at 2:00 in the morning and took a taxi to the Bronx. He stopped off at a 24-hour liquor store near Fordham and sat down under a leafless, lifeless tree on campus and started to drink. For October, the air was very extremely chilly. He stood up as if on some mission and started to walk, holding the bottle of bourbon in a paper sack in one hand.

The area around the Poe cottage looked like he felt: dark, isolated, derelict. The pavement was cracked and slightly buckled in places. Most of the street lamps had been broken out, but the daytime shuffle of pedestrians and traffic had cleared most of the glass away, except the one piece, it seemed, the one stuck to his shoe. He continued to walk. He needed to get drunk again, but drunkenness eluded him, even though the bottle was almost empty. Henry walked a deliberate and steady pace, listening to the slight swishing of the contents of his bottle and to the sounds of Roz's voice echoing in his head.

Henry didn't expect locked gates at the cottage. He decided to climb over them but his shoe got caught. Taking the shoe off, the piece of glass embedded itself into the bottom of his left ring finger, but it did not bleed. Henry made his way to the cottage door.

Locked? He truly seemed surprised. "Aren't we family?!" Henry yelled into the night. He pounded the door, but nobody answered. "Virginia? Eddie? Oh, hell." Henry turned around and allowed his body to slide down the length of the front door. He quickly finished the bottle of Heaven Hill and loudly started to recite some of the lines from Annabel Lee:

"I was a child and she was a child,
    In this kingdom by the sea,
But we loved with a love that was more than love—
    I and my Annabel Lee—
With a love that the wingèd seraphs of Heaven
    Coveted her and me.

But our love it was stronger by far than the love
    Of those who were older than we—
    Of many far wiser than we—
And neither the angels in Heaven above . . ."

Henry paused and pounded his chest as he recited the rest.

"Nor the demons down under the sea

Can ever dissever my soul from the soul

Of the beautiful Annabel Lee"

Falling over to his side and before drifting into an alcoholic slumber, Henry raised his empty bottle and spoke to it: "The seraphins killed her, my friend.. No, no, no, no, no, NO!

The seraphins killed us . . . Sera . . . phina."

Henry woke to the sound of car horns on the busy streets surrounding the park.

He felt a sense of urgency. He needed to get back to Roz and make her know he understood what had come between them. He didn't know how to accomplish this—but he felt he must.

Desperation can kill you, but sometimes it is the very thing that can make things right.

Henry remembered Roz telling him about an antique store near the Botanical Gardens. He decided to go there and find a sugar spoon for Roz's tea service, the only piece missing from her tea service.

Henry walked over to Fordham and flagged down a couple students. Finally, he came across a rather somber professor who knew the store but seemed a bit concerned about a disheveled man insisting on directions to a rather high-end store. Henry ignored the man's stares and went off to take the bus. He found the store but stopped first across the street to a Rite Aid. He was aware of his appearance, so he purchased a comb and some aftershave and asked to freshen up in the restroom. Henry then went into the store and pulled out the money clip Roz had given him for his first Father's Day. Although he loved it, he remembered how he teased her: "Fine gift for a socialist, Roz! I don't have enough dollar bills to share." He smiled. What a happy day it was.

"Well, hopefully, it is enough for a spoon," he thought. To his dismay, the owner had no silver sugar spoons. Henry placed his hands on the display and lowered his head. In the case, he noticed an antique gun box. May I see this? The silver plate on the top and its engraved words caught his eye, "Divine Providence," Henry read aloud.

"A man brought this in a few months ago. Said it was a family piece. I don't know why it says that on the front. That's a Chippendale-style ...mahogany case ...1800s."

Opening it, the shopkeeper said, "No guns were in it, and the wool lining is torn. I don't know why I accepted it. For some reason, it seemed charming."

"It is charming. I love it. I think I can turn this into a jewelry box for my wife. She's in Providence right now."

The owner laughed. "Are you sure you want to buy your wife a case like this one? This likely held two dueling pistols, you know. Maybe the English flintlock kind."

"That makes it even more perfect."

Henry took the case back to his hotel. He opened the box, and started to remove the blue wool lining. "I can probably get some velvet or something and glue that on." Henry did not know what he was doing really, but he felt, whatever it was, it was right. The lining proved to be difficult to remove, but, when he did, he noticed a handwritten letter. The day was illegible—a small spot of red sealing wax had spoiled it— but October and 1847 and Providence were still legible. It was not addressed to anyone nor signed by anyone. Only a small hand-drawn lyre appeared at the bottom of the page.

"I write to you on this lonesome October, this lonesome anniversary." Henry wept as he read the words of this unknown woman to the man she loved but could not have. In it, she spoke of pistols: "It is such Divine Providence the pistols did not arrive on time . . ."

It seems dueling pistols had been ordered by the woman's husband, but they had not arrived on time, allowing the object of the letter and the object of this woman's affections to escape. It apparently had given her husband time to reconsider, as well.

The woman insisted he was not a coward but a good man to honor his vows and to care for his sick wife. His actions, she wrote, were not to blame for the loss of their child, this darling angel watching them from the heavens. She implored him to accept this gift of the dueling pistols and to admire their beauty. She hoped he would understand their symbol.

What should have been "life-taking" became "life-giving." Perhaps their child's death, she wrote, was also for the purpose of preserving life and reputation. Perhaps they would meet and love again, "not forgetting the past in some sweet Lethean slumbers," but honoring and respecting the past and forgiving. She wrote a lot about forgiveness and about time.

On the train back to Providence, Henry noted it was the 7th of October. Had he been in Baltimore, he would have paid his respects at the Poe grave, but nothing was important as this . . . He rushed along from the train station up to Benefit Street, not even knowing if Roz was still there. When he arrived at the apartment, he knocked. At first, she didn't hear him. She was listening to Van Morrison . . .

I will walk out of the darkness
And I'll walk into the light
And I'll sing the song of ages
And the dawn will end the night

Feel the angel of the present
In the mighty crystal fire

Lift me up consume my darkness
Let me travel even higher

Henry knocked a bit louder, and Roz answered the door. She looked sad and told Henry she was packing and had a flight to catch to New Orleans. Henry told Roz he understood, and he would not fight the annulment. He asked her to accept one last gift in honor of their happier times, in honor of the love they had shared and the love they had created.

Roz opened the beautiful wooden box after running her fingers over the letters on the silver plate. She looked quizzically at Henry when she saw the old letter inside. "Just read it, please. I'll explain later." A tear ran down Henry's face.

As she read the letter, Rosalind's hands began to shake. She fell into Henry's arms. "This," she paused and looked up at Henry, "This is our angel. This is what we have needed, isn't it?" She relaxed as Henry wrapped his arms around her, and let out a small sigh when he whispered to her "It's our story." She wrapped her arms around his waist, put her head on his shoulder, and wept.

"Love pulls us from the past into the future. From there you can go anywhere you want, forward or back. Anywhere, Roz. Truth and love are the only two things that matter in life."

"There are a couple more things," Roz said, "and they're right here in the present."

CASE FOR FLINTLOCK DUELING PISTOLS

Cecelia, Dancer, Suffers Drawbacks
But Returns to the Streets, Well-armed

Elisavietta Ritchie

Eye swollen shut, no scarves will veil. Can't be seen today or go to work. They'll ask, "He at it again?"

If I stay home, only dumb TV—sitcoms, detective, boxing—all where guys with black eyes end up on their duffs.

Or I'd have to clean closets: clear gowns tattered from years in the spotlights of hell…

Ah! My coverall crème, lipstick, powder, mascara, rouge, eye shadow so the both eyes match. I'll make up, doll up, return to the streets, and my subterranean lives, celebrate my dark mysterious eyes…

But beware! One-eyed, my mother-of-pearl custom-made Ladysmith can still shoot and shoot straight, and I get what I want.

Goin' Huntin' with my Uncle

Elisavietta Ritchie

"A poem about your favorite sport?" I suggested to the fourth-grader, who seemed stymied by my earlier ideas flung out in the hope something might inspire the class.

"Goin' huntin' now deer-season's finally opened." He preferred to write prose but would try writing in stanzas. "Last night we cleaned our guns. Brownings and Bushmasters—"

I feared squelching any glimmer of creativity, which as a poet-in-the-schools I was supposed to jumpstart…"Also write a poem from the viewpoint of the deer…Two poems side by side…?"

He pondered more. Since other students were deep in writing poems from the viewpoints of diverse critters as well as "What if George Washington were transported to the Present World," he began wear down the borrowed Ticonderoga #2…

No way to retrieve his name, but I remember enough of his poem to reconstruct our own.

A Doe Presents Her Side of the Argument

"No argument, Boy, I'm paralyzed with fear,
can't dash away as fast as my cousins–
They flick their tails, leap your fence, find safer woods.
My hoof caught in a mole trap hurts—
Please drop that gun!

You clench it all the harder,
I hear the click as you cock—
Please spare my life!

All summer you did not know
I watched you through the leaves.
Now leaves falling away, catch on
my long eyelashes as on your short ones,
we watch each other—Could be friends—

When you were small and so was I
you wanted me for a pet like your cat.
Yet now we're both bigger you would shoot me—

I guess shooting is what you humans do.
Nights I've slipped up to your house,
peered in windows, seen you watch
flicker-pictures with murders, wars—

I've watched you leave dressed up to pray—
Does your god want you to kill?
You say God looks after sparrows;
we deer have flesh more like your own.

You lack elegant fur and long eyelashes
but we all bleed, and even after we die.
I've seen humans attack dead flanks with knives,
toss bones in the swamp for foxes to gnaw.

Goin' Huntin' with my Uncle

Please spare my life!
I promise not to eat more lettuce, spinach, kale.
I will eat all your poison ivy.
Drop that gun!

My Father's Gun

Mike Luster

That nude
of Marilyn
on red satin
hung inside
his closet door,
the gate
to his place
of secrets
where he kept
dice, cards,
a cigarette roller,
a homemade dagger,
and in the corner
a .22 rifle
lethal, alluring.
Texas 1963.
he died
before Kennedy
that year
a stroke
not a shot
His gun
now a secret
in my closet
hidden from
young sons
no bullet
in the house.

Hawk Look

Excerpt from "Two Birds I Shot"

Jim Terr

Way back in New Mexico.
About 30 or 40 years ago.
I used to go out hunting dove
(Yes, you heard right—the bird of love.)

With no idea what I was doing
So I did not cut short much cooing.
But one day I brought down a hawk.
He fell to earth without a yawp.

A neighbor into taxidermy
Mounted him quite nicely for me.
And so he stared at me for years.
(If I had doubts, I did not hear.)

Only now I feel disturbed
And wonder how his look reverb'd
Inside my skull. And so I wonder
If he still does drag me under.

The Hunt

Michael Gibbons

Sitting in my stand
high in the oak
deer trail down below
no deer

Waiting, watching
seeing red fox catch mice
in the field stone wall
no deer

Red hawks gliding
swooping
I sit in my stand
no deer

Something out there
running
coyote fairly dancing
no deer

Sitting in my stand
I admire
no deer

The Gun as Medium

When Andy Warhol Got Shot

Mariah Fox

Andy Warhol was pronounced dead six minutes after he arrived in the Columbus Hospital emergency room. It was June 4, 1968, and it had been less than an hour since Valerie Solanis shot Warhol with a handgun at his Factory art studio in New York City. On the way to the hospital, it was suggested that Leo Castelli, Andy's art dealer, would surely pay the extra $15 for the sirens to be switched on during the drive so the ambulance could go faster, (in addition to hinting at collectors that Warhol works might be suddenly much more valuable moving forward). Upon his arrival, when doctors saw the shot's damage, Warhol heard them saying, "Forget it..." and, "...no chance." *The New York Post* churned out a headline: "Andy Warhol Fights for Life."

It was a slice of real-life Pop art drama playing out– an everyday 1960s narration of rebellion and violence, happening in real-time action. This time, it was a famous artist getting shot. Pop pioneer Andy Warhol was always fascinated with news like this! In this particular piece, a .32 automatic appeared to be the medium of choice, Solanis the shooter, and Andy was the subject. One day later, Robert Kennedy would also be shot, and sadly, fatally wounded. The media news of Kennedy's assassination transfixed and confused Warhol and he thought it was John all over again. He called it a "strange rerun" after lasting his own 5-hour life-saving surgery, and drifting through the pain-filled stupors of early recovery: "I just thought, after you die, they rerun things for you...I couldn't distinguish between life and death yet..."

Warhol lived to survive, and later described Valerie Solanis' attempt at his life with extreme lucidity. He easily noted that the troubled Solanis was exhibiting what we might call nowadays, serious "cray," as she rode up the elevator with him and stepped into The Factory. He recalled that she wore layers of hot winter clothing on a very warm summer day but didn't sweat, and repeatedly twisted the neck of the brown paper bag she carried, while bouncing on the balls of her feet. No one knew that inside the brown bag was her address book, a Kotex maxi-pad, a .32 automatic, and an extra gun just in case, a .22 revolver. (Though she'd paid $65 for the .32, she didn't trust it).

Andy Warhol was frequently known to be a difficult guy. The self-motivated "business artist" could haggle and specify relentlessly to such a degree that he was at times, unbearable to deal with in person. He knew what he was interested in, and what he did not care for. Andy had previously been unresponsive to Valerie Solanis' requests for money in compensation for a script proposal that had become lost in the Factory, and her soon to be published, male race-extermination scheme book, the *SCUM Manifesto*. This frustrated her. When he first met her, Warhol, who was ever fascinated by unusual people, had initially thought that Solanis might be a "dirty lady cop," and was turned off. She had written what Warhol described as "dirty" scripts that he wasn't interested in producing. But she'd persisted to show up in his crowd, she'd acted well in one of his film scenes, and he had kind of gotten used to her popping up…

The disgruntled Solanis began by firing two shots, but missed. By then, Warhol was the first to realize what was taking place, and yelled "No! Don't do it!" He collapsed in panic on the floor to hide (but instead trapped himself) beneath a glass desk. The third bullet entered Warhol's stomach from close range on the right. It proceeded to puncture a lung, and ricochet through his esophagus, gall bladder, spleen, liver and intestines, coming out the other side. He lay there and began to bleed.

Later, the police would have plenty of people to interview about the crime scene. Just moments before the painful shot, Andy had been chatting on the phone with Viva, who was telling him all about her hair color for an upcoming scene in the big new counterculture Hollywood film, *Midnight Cowboy* starring Jon Voigt. Viva could hear the shots over the phone line, and at first, she thought someone in the room nearby was cracking the old whip from their Velvet Underground stage days.

A number of others close to Warhol fled the room, and helped to hold adjacent doors closed tight, keeping Solanis from roaming further with her gun. After firing a few more shots, and trying but failing to find those who were hiding behind locked doors, Solanis decided to flee the scene, leaving her brown paper bag on the desk. Billy Name, caretaker of the Factory, was developing photos in the back, and one of the first to be with Andy after the danger had passed, crying over him. Andy said it hurt immensely, and that he couldn't breathe. Minutes later, Warhol's right hand, poet, screen-print man (and Velvet Underground whip-handler) Gerard Malanga walked in, then took off immediately. Andy's mother adored Gerard; and he wanted to intercept and inform Mrs. Warhola that her son was hurt before someone else did; she and Andy were very close and this was clearly serious.

Andy Warhol had a working class immigrant's gene pool— he had already nearly passed on at least once, being born a sickly child in cold, poverty-stricken 1920s Pittsburgh. His parents were peasants who had immigrated from Ruthenia in the Carpathian Mountains (now Ukraine); Warhol and his siblings knew the rough life, the street, the city, and about survival. Andy had been a frail boy who drew pictures to help himself through the isolation he felt during near-fatal childhood illness. His talent, unique artistic style and determination carried him on a full ride through college. After graduation from Carnegie Mellon, he experienced commercial success in New York, making his way as a successful art director and illustrator in the 1950s, before hitting the blue-chip gallery scene with his controversial Campbell Soup cans and celebrity screen prints, which marked art history forevermore. Warhol's art has always captured moments from life that somehow make an impression, whether they be heroic, mundane, purposeful, purposeless, beautiful, magnetic, disturbing, confusing, careless, silly, meaningless, narcissistic, humble, familial, dark, naughty or playful.

Warhol enjoyed the act of living: he sought delight, stimulation, creative success, and the ability to explore the world along with his faithful entourage. It seems, that the attempt on his life with a .32 automatic is just another fascinating chapter in the life of Andy Warhol. The savage bullet didn't lay him out, though from his pale, frail looks, it should have. He went on to work for nearly 20 more years after the shooting. The following summer Richard Avedon, the master portrait photographer, shot Andy's torso in a leather jacket pulled aside to reveal his hideous scars, looking romantic, and eerily powerful. Interestingly, when later recalling the time "when he was getting shot," it seemed to trouble Andy the most that he had already filmed counterculture stories about forbidden subjects like hustlers years before *Midnight Cowboy* came out and he asked, "Why didn't they give us the money... We would have done it so real for them?"

Still, Warhol was deeply affected by the attempt on his art-life with a gun-medium. He wrote in his journals that he began to reconsider everyone he knew that had ever carried a gun, and how previously, that had seemed unreal. But clearly the pain made this time different, and very real. One thing that he noticed sharply, was the strange look in Solanis' eye that day: "Crazy people had always fascinated me because they were so creative—they were incapable of doing things normally.

Usually, they would never hurt anybody, they were just disturbed themselves; but how would I ever know again which was which? ...The fear of getting shot again made me think that I'd never again enjoy talking to somebody whose eyes looked weird..."

The police detectives rifled through Warhol's space for hours, taping areas off and looking for clues, spilling transparencies of flowers, movie stills and old receipts, making a mess amidst protests from the Factory's caretakers. The very last place the police decided to look was the twisted, brown paper bag atop the desk that Warhol had hidden under, still containing a gun, the Kotex and address book. Jackpot!? Shortly afterward, Solanis turned herself in and admitted to the crime. She served months in prison for her bad behavior, during which time Warhol continued to fear for his life, especially when she was released around two years later.

Meanwhile when Bob Rauschenberg, another (sometimes) infamous Pop artist, heard the news at Max's about the shootings after dancing heavily, he collapsed on the floor sobbing, and cried, "Is this the medium?" When Andy heard about Bob's reaction, he asked, "What was that supposed to mean?" The response: "First you, then Bobby Kennedy. Guns."

After being shot with a .32 automatic, Andy Warhol was clinically dead for one and a half minutes after arrival in the emergency room. It was summer, 1968.

Works Cited: Channing, Will. "Untitled Conversation." Personal interview. 9 Jan. 2016. Warhol, Andy, and Pat Hackett. *POPism: The Warhol Sixties*. Orlando: Harcourt, 2006. Print. Watson, Steven. *Factory Made: Warhol and the Sixties*. New York: Pantheon, 2003. Print.

By the Gun

A Sudden Story

Bob Arnold

Funny that you should ask about Van Gogh and a gun. Some believe he was actually shot by two passing teens, boys, who liked to rile the young artist at work. Vincent was the parade of marauders simply by the way he lived, looked, and went about his days traipsing the village with an easel over his back, paints splashed on his cheeks since he was also known to eat his paints, never mind the wild red hair and the wilder look. Perfect target for bullies. It happened. So instead of Van Gogh shooting himself as a suicide, some believe these two rascals got into a thing with Vincent out in the field and sunny pastures of plenty of his work, took his gun in a tussle and shot the artist. Vincent being Vincent decided not to press charges, let the whole thing go, maybe the idea of dying was okay finally to him, he'd had enough of life and living and he'll just light his pipe in bed and leak out all the blood in his body. The doctor who came to administer relief told Vincent's brother Theo and the irritable patient that he could save his life and the artist said something like, "What? so I can do it all over again!" What a guy. He would die. His beloved brother always by his side would die six months afterwards. Both too young to die but die they did.

In Vincent's case, it was by the gun.

Young Hearts

Trent Zelazny

There were around fifty of them.

Some spun on the merry-go-round, others see-sawed on teeter-totters, slid down towering slides, swung up and down on swing-sets, or climbed across monkey bars. A few bored teachers stood around, too, apparently playing *Guess Who's Sleeping.*

It was eight minutes past ten in the morning.

So many of the little runts fit perfectly within the crosshairs of his scope, which was attached to his Savage MK II bolt action rifle, with its gleaming stainless-steel action and barrel, its hardwood stock. While practicing, he'd been surprised at how astoundingly accurate it was. The piece was far more upscale than its price tag had indicated.

Holstered at either hip was a Bersa Thunder, each featuring two ambidextrous safety controls, reversible magazine releases, automatic firing pin safety, adjustable trigger stops, and combat-style skeletonized hammers. Each pistol was equipped with an extended magazine, which held nine rounds of 9mm ammunition. He had extra ammo with him.

His name didn't matter. He was thirty-seven years old, divorced, and lived alone.

The small stream he'd crossed to get here had slightly dampened his foot. Touching his shoe, he then touched the butt of the pistol hipped on his right, then touched it again, then once more and rubbed his fingers together before bringing his hand back up to the rifle's grip.

He looked through the scope again. Right in the middle was a woman, one of the teachers, pretty and probably close to his own age, light brown hair tinted with red, a blue cardigan, tight-fitting jeans. She looked bored beyond belief.

But there was a lot of laughter down there.

And like always, here he was, alone, tucked clandestine within the trees. For almost two years he'd been thinking about this, and for the last two weeks he'd planned it down to the last detail, looking at it from every possible angle. While there is never ever a guarantee, it was basically foolproof. And if it wasn't, if there was something he'd over-looked, then fuck it.

Through an indignantly retrospective fog a doctor spoke of his men-tal health. Depression, avoiding contact with other people, unaddressed anger, PTSD, becoming increasingly fearful. His ex-wife had regularly referred to him as "mentally unhinged" toward the end of their marriage. Said there were a million examples of his irrational behavior and illog-ical thought process. Yeah, like she had all of her faculties in place.

Bitch.

He would've loved to be "a normal person." He would've loved to shed the anger that caused him, from time to time, to act out in aggres-sive ways. But just what in the world was normal, anyway? Very little he'd ever come across.

A blond girl on one of the swings wailed like a happy banshee. The man made her the center of attention, slid his finger off the trigger guard and began to ease it over the trigger proper. Then he stopped, remained perfectly still.

He wasn't trembling. Wasn't shaking at all. He was steady as a sur-geon, and that did not sit well with him. He'd been diagnosed with Essential Tremor over twenty years ago. He always trembled a little, but he wasn't now.

Was he finally being released from some of his life-long ailments? Was this decision, indeed, somehow, a cleansing one?

He did not believe in God. If there was a god, he wouldn't be where he was at this moment, staring through the scope of a rifle at a bunch of grade schoolers. He would still be married, still have a job, he would be more in control without so much lunacy constantly assaulting his mind, and if not great, his life would likely pass for at least pedestrian—maybe even a tad benign.

But there was no god.

He closed his eyes, opened them, and focused on the little blond girl again. She'd moved, hopped off the swing and was running around with a group of other kids who were getting ready to play some kind of game, Simon Says or Freeze Tag or something.

It would be simple to just…

It was like hearing vibrations inside his skull. Hazy vapor whited out the scope and washed out the surrounding trees and rocks he'd settled himself within. He crouched in mist, which swirled and maneuvered around him in chimera-like swooshes, fluctuating within itself from white to gray, black to blue to red to white, some of it taking on shapes, some of it creating windows and doorways, though most of it simply lingered, hovering mesmeric in the air about him.

Someone's gonna answer for what happened. That's what the old man always said, reeking of liquor. *Someone's gonna answer.*

Out of the haze stepped the old man, belt already drawn from his jeans and folded once in half.

Mom! Mommy! Help me! But all that drugged-out cunt ever did was light another cigarette and watch her stupid television shows, except for the time he was on the floor, covered in welts and with a black eye and twisted ankle, and she told him to get her another beer.

A tear tickled the edge of his eye, but he couldn't tell if it was real or imagined. Everything was both, simultaneously, it seemed.

Faces peeped through the nebulous windows. Shapeless entities roamed around him as abstract forms entered, left, or stood within foggy entryways.

Just visible through it all was the school, the playground, the children playing. His finger had moved back up to the trigger guard and perspiration condensated on his flesh as the mist dispersed.

They looked so happy. So carefree. So young. These kids had... decent childhoods?

The little bastards. *He* didn't get one of those. Never even got a say in the matter. All he got was born to a couple of assholes who would've rather he not exist. Except he *did* exist, whether they liked it or not—and they did not.

The old man was dead, and good riddance. Beaten to death by a group of marines outside a bar. No doubt the bastard had it coming, and at least he'd been executed in a militaristic way.

Mom was still alive, a binge-drinking, chain-smoking, pill-popping recluse. Her mind had never been fully functional, as far as he could recall, and it had been getting worse and worse the last few years. There were times when she didn't even know who he was, on the rare occasions he visited.

On one of those visits he confronted his mother about his childhood, the beatings, the abuse, the neglect. Mom told him he was making it all up. According to her, they were good parents.

He brought his eye away from the scope, winced as pain like hot coals tumbled around his sternum, some dropping into his stomach, a few bouncing up into his chest, which grew heavy, as though kettlebells had been hooked to his heart. His body oscillated but his hands remained steady.

A wave of anger rose in the undulating ocean of feeling natant inside him. It crashed down and a muscle spasm jerked his back. His head snapped like he'd sneezed, and his eyelids flickered with rapid blinks. He drew a deep breath, held it, exhaled.

After a time, what must be reality returned to him. No fog to shroud anything. Just the school, the spiritless teachers, the children, running, screaming, laughing, playing Freeze Tag.

Eye back to the scope, he watched it all for a time, disregarding the cross wire. Watched the frenetic joy of little children scampering, hopping, smiling.

Once upon a time he'd scampered and hopped. Last time he did that he was probably five, maybe six years old. His desire to play had been knocked out of him, because someone had to answer.

Someone always has to answer. It's a law of life, though laws for life are cryptic at best. State and federal laws were even worse. Orwell's *1984* was what the state of things was becoming. No one, not even law enforcement or politicians, were clear on what the laws were, or how they were meant to work, but give someone a badge and, even if they're a dim-witted asshole, they will enforce whatever misrepresented regulations they're instructed to. The badge gives them license to enforce whatever law, true or false, by whatever means they deem necessary—or feel like—with minimal risk of consequences—even when a dozen or more people catch their actions on video.

Justice had become illusory, imponderable, the badge symbolic of abuse within despotism.

Crazy bastards, all of them.

Everyone hates politicians, but they always vote to put them in office. The man didn't vote. He saw no point. People kept voting for these imbeciles with only one true thing in their hearts: ignorant hope. They forget that all of them have been terrible, and will continue to be.

Idiots. A country, a world of idiots…

Far beyond time for a revolution. Hell, maybe too late.

But actions could still be taken. Some say actions speak louder than words. His rifle would speak much louder than his voice could ever hope to.

Why do people keep producing these little creatures? Haven't they figured out that all they're doing is bringing life into a world where they can only be destroyed, ruined, crushed?

Life was no longer meant for the living.

A lonesome boy played by himself in the sizable sandbox, off to the man's right. He wore a dusty Star Wars T-shirt, blue roll-up pants, and sandals. He had created small mountains. Occasionally he looked up at the other kids, then turned his head down and slumped further, before returning to his mountainous landscape. Even from this distance, the man saw a tiny frown on the boy's face.

The man's eyes squeezed shut tight as his eyeballs tried to pop out of their sockets. He couldn't count how times he'd been that little boy....

Alone in his room, some tattered comic books and thrift store toys and second-hand clothes his only possessions. Lying on his back on the splintery, uneven floorboards covered solely by a threadbare oval rug, staring up at the ceiling, which once upon a time had probably been beige, now a darker brown from years of cigarette smoke wafting through the house.

Hands behind his head, he listened to the music coming from the living room. The Statler Brothers, "My Only Love." He had to adjust his hearing in order to hear the song through the cries and beating also coming from the living room.

Knowing it was only a matter of time....

He brought his eye away from the scope again, this time with a flinch. That poor boy down there in the sandbox was going to end up just like him. The man wondered if he should take the kid out first, last, or if he should even take him out at all. It was all guesswork, what the man was thinking. He wondered if the kid in the Star Wars shirt was ever hit, if maybe he had a bullying older sibling, or mother or father. He wondered if the kid sat alone in his room most of the time, afraid to go out, or if he got pushed around so much at school that he now separated himself from the pack as a means of survival.

All life is precious.

Someone told him that once, though he couldn't recall who.

A few of the kids had put together a little soft ball game. The man did not know how to throw a ball, or swing a bat. More often than not he'd been picked last for any sort of athletics.

The boy in the sandbox looked at the game, then turned down again and wiped out his landscape. Dismay over the collapse was so great that the man wanted to leave flowers in the sandbox as a tribute.

Dust still rose from the disintegrated piles and peaks. There was a cloud around the boy when the softball thudded into the box two feet from him.

"Jeremy," a kid in a baseball cap said, voice faint due to distance.

The kid in the sandbox took hold of the ball, contemplated it, and slowly got to his feet. He located the boy playing umpire, lifted his leg to the point where his thigh became parallel with the ground, broke his arms in a downward semi-circular motion, lowered his leg and strode outwards, extending his pitching arm as far as he could and letting the ball glide off his wrist.

Invisible as it flew through the air, the ball smacked the umpire's glove with a heavy thud, sending the umpire, who was in stance, back a step.

Everyone on the playground froze. The man froze, too. This little nobody kid had just performed a miracle; had just pitched a ball as fast and as accurate as they do in the big leagues.

Something inside the man quaked. He could have sworn he'd been that little boy a million times over. But he'd never been capable of anything as amazing as that. How old was Jeremy, anyway? Nine, ten?

All life is precious.

Untrue. The man's life was not. Maybe somehow that little boy's life was precious, but not his. Had it been, it would have been nurtured, his days would not have been spent in hiding, or in beatings—in answering. And whether or not he ever had a talent like that Jeremy kid down there, the man was never allowed to discover it. He never even had a chance. Maybe he could have become a miracle worker, too, but in the end he became just another loser.

Was it his fault? No, at least not entirely, but he certainly didn't help himself any. All that old stuff had become the predominant ingredient in his mental, emotional and physical makeup, and alone, hiding as much as he did, dwelling on it all, only ingrained such turmoil further into his psyche.

My only love...

Jeremy had a chance. He'd just proven that. That momentary magic completely separated the man from the kid in the sandbox, who was now up and being included in the game. And like always, here he was, alone, tucked clandestine within the trees.

Maybe it's not them; maybe it's you, a doctor, a therapist, a whack job once told him. A therapist who had always been judgmental of his behavior, who didn't appear to take him seriously, and who tried to manipulate his feelings, inducing guilt or making him feel bad about his behavior and emotions. A therapist who should've had his license revoked.

Maybe it's you.

Of course it was him! But it was everyone else, too. Everyone in the world was an apathetic, uncaring, sociopathic, psychopathic, manipulative creep, indulging in activities such as xenophobia, discrimination, and bigotry. Some folks were blessed with fancy flights of good deeds, and the occasional genuine good soul did grace the planet. But fear, and hate—those were the major two that kept the world moving as it did, yet it could not continue progressing in this fashion for much longer.

And these children—the prescription on his eyes must have suddenly changed. Innocent, carefree, happy, performing exemplary feats, laughing together—these kids were what the world *could* be. If they could keep from getting squashed, if they could bend the world to their whim rather than the other way around, maybe, just maybe there could be a chance…

The man realized something. His lip quivered but nothing else moved.

He had no right to take away the future, not the future of the world or of a single other. These children still had lives, and if nurtured, if things went okay for them, then maybe the future could indeed be just a little bit brighter.

These kids had lives.

The man did not.

He rose to his feet—

Let the young hearts go their way.

—and slung the rifle over his shoulder.

Maybe it's not them; maybe it's you.

Or maybe it's all of us.

The man turned and walked away from the school, staring down at his feet, traversing over rocks and dips and shrubs. His car was half a mile away. Between it and himself was the small stream he'd crossed when he'd initially come to destroy that which he no longer felt he had any right to destroy.

Young hearts can go their way. I'll go mine. I won't interfere.

He came to the stream, crouched down and looked into the slow running water that flowed through and over the knobby stones at the bottom, saw a dull and indistinct but sad reflection looking back at him.

It's not my place. I don't get to decide for others…

Still staring into the stream, he let the rifle fall from his shoulder, listened to the stock punch the dirt then the whole thing clatter to the ground. The liquefied face in the water had answered and answered but had never come up with any answers of its own.

Sometimes, it's just the way it goes.

"Good luck, Jeremy," he said softly, hearing defeat in his tone.

Those kids had a chance at a life. The man's chance had come and gone. He was nothing now. But those back there… there was… it was almost as though…

The man's life was over. There was no future for him, even if he wanted there to be one. If there had ever been a time for him, it had ended long ago.

But let the young hearts go their way…

His aqueous eyelids blinked.

And keep going, kid. Don't let what happened to me happen to you…

Staring at his rippling reflection, the man reached to his right hip and eased out the pistol holstered there.

BERSA THUNDER 9MM
PISTOL WITH EXTENDED
MAGAZINE

The Knife is Sharper than the Gun

Brigham Hausman

Sometimes stealth and elegance have more effect than sheer power.

The events in question all happened back in my days of working behind the bar. Specifically, they occurred around the cusp of graduating from bar-back to bartender. At the time I was barely 21, but legit nonetheless. I had a real ID and no longer needed to memorize a different astrological sign to prove my birth date. My mentor bartender, Ben, wanted to celebrate his birthday in San Jose. Many people residing in Santa Cruz were not too keen on San Jose, inclined to say it was full of kooks. I was a University student, and therefore already a bit of an outcast by local standards for that crime so I was willing to go if transportation was not my responsibility. At that point, it was unwise to make anything but drinking and bedding cocktail waitresses my responsibility.

Ben, having already gotten his driving privileges revoked by the state a year earlier, got the driving part covered by his friend from high school, who would later that evening reveal himself a major shit-head. Impressive considering he was up against me and Ben in that department. I don't remember this friend's real name, which says a lot considering how effective my memory normally is, but let's call him Dolph for the sake of clarity.

So Ben and I finish our shifts, him tending, me backing, both of us drinking about as much as we are giving away to our friends in exchange for enhanced cash tips. Bar staff in their twenties residing in a surf/college town did not work sober unless they were too hung over to hold down a shot, so we were already toasty when we headed over the Hill.

I rode in the back of a pickup truck, illegal in California, yes, but surreptitious because it had a camper shell over the bed. Ha! Try to tell US what to do, will you? Highway 17 wound through the hills and we took it at high speeds, on wet pavement with a driver who had enjoyed the benefits of being in our "in" crowd while we were working. It seemed like a reasonable way to get around at the time. I really didn't care about the potential hazards because I found myself preoccupied by the fact that I had to urinate very badly indeed. Every sweeping turn made my bloated bladder slosh painfully.

At one point an empty screw-top bottle bounced into me and I managed to relieve a bit of the pressure with a minimum of distribution of used liquids throughout the back of the truck by way of filling the vessel back up. We finally got into the Valley and parked. It was probably the longest 60 minutes of my life. It felt even longer than 60 seconds of boxing feels when you run out of gas and spend it eating punches. When the truck stopped, I burst out of the back and charged off to create a minor illegal flood zone, urinating in public for at least two minutes without stopping.

We headed to some cheesy night club, namely the Oasis Ballroom, and started getting more fucked up to properly celebrate Ben's birthday while unsuccessfully trying to meet San Jose chicks.

The night passed relatively quickly and a few hours later I discovered last call upon us. I had managed to drink away almost all of the tips I earned during my shift earlier that night. I found myself alone, waiting at one of the bars in the place, annoyed that it took so long to order another drink. Time and time again the tender gave preferential service to San Jose locals over me even though I had been tipping extravagantly all night.

Bartender secret handshake rule: When you work in bar service, you tip your fellow tenders well and they're supposed to reciprocate by at least getting drinks to you fast, preferably on the cheap as well, but fast is a great starting point. By the time this guy got around to me, I was pretty irked. Apparently he forgot to review the rule book before coming to work.

After I paid for my drink I had two dollars left to my name. Normally, I would have left them both on the bar for the tender but his final service ranked so poorly I was tempted to leave no tip at all. This was and still is considered a CARDINAL sin among bartenders, regardless of the motivation, and I could not reconcile it so I capitulated and split the difference, leaving one dollar on the bar and taking my other last, bitter greenback with me. I was drunk enough to have trouble walking around stationary objects like tables without an occasional collision, and I still thought it was silly to hang onto a single, basically worthless dollar. However, considering the principles involved, it felt like my best option.

I caught up with Ben and Dolph and, shoving my solitary dollar back into my pocket, headed to the ride with them. As we walked towards the parking lot, I saw two guys about 15 feet ahead of us talking and glancing back at us. Bright mercury-halide lights shown off the rain slick pavement, illuminating the concrete walls outside of the club and I could clearly see the two of them, dressed like they had been out clubbing, too: collared shirts, slacks, well groomed, not sketchy looking at all. It felt almost like broad daylight and I did not sense any threat coming from them.

Until they stopped and turned to face the three of us. The one on the right brandished a knife and the one on the left held a chrome plated .25 caliber Beretta. I thought to myself, "Great, I have one fucking dollar. I'd have been better off giving it to the useless bartender back at the club. Now I'll probably get shot for it."

I saw Ben take all the money out of his pocket and hand it to the guy with the knife. My turn. I got amused by the dark irony of the situation. These guys were risking serious jail time for a single stinking buck. I reached into my pocket and withdrew my solitary bill, handing it to the guy with the pistol.

He took it, looked down at what he received and then looked back at me, incredulous. He thrust the gun towards me again, poking the air between us with the barrel as if I had somehow missed the gravity of the situation. I wondered if he was going to pull the trigger to prove his point, but what the fuck could I do? I had just given him everything I had.

I shrugged, smirked and put my hands back in my pockets, waiting for him to make his move. In the mean time Dolph handed Mr. Knife about six dollars and as Knife took the money, Dolph the dumb-ass made a grab for the knife, like some sort of misguided action hero in a movie. Luckily, instead of provoking the gun wielder to shoot us, Knife simply yanked his blade free, slicing Dolph's hand handsomely in the process, and then bailing with his gun toting friend.

The pistol may not have been loaded. I have since heard charges are less severe for using an unloaded firearm to relieve people of their pocket cash. Meanwhile the knife had made its statement quickly, silently and efficiently. No law enforcement got alerted to our mishap until after we made it to the emergency room.

Getting treatment for Dolph took agonizingly long, even for a busy Saturday night. I had had enough personal emergency room experience to know this for a fact. The hospital, annoyingly, had no beer vendors to help pass the time in a more civilized fashion.

The next day, Ben came into the bar to nurse his hangover while I worked. Ben gave a good explanation for the delay at the hospital. Even punchy and tired from getting home at 7AM with just enough time to lay down for an hour, get up, shower, get on my bike and ride back to work for my consistently ball-busting, cheap tipping Sunday AM shift, I found myself marveling at the unmitigated extent of Dolph's stupidity.

For six dollars he had risked all three of our lives, but, apparently an overachiever in his own right, Dolph had to take it to the next level. While waiting for a doctor to look at him, he chose to explain to an African American nurse that the twin 'SS' riveted into his black leather jacket represented his affiliation with the white Aryan racist community, effectively bumping him to the bottom of the priority treatment list for hours. Decision making skills like this go a long way in explaining the beliefs and actions of his constituents.

Yes, the knife is sharper than the gun and sometimes it thinks quicker than the bullet.

Timmy is Gone

Peter Eichstaedt

A whiff of smoke curled from the barrel of the gun. It was heavy in Roger's hand as he held it sideways and examined it, his ears still ringing from the shot. He lowered the gun and let it hang, pointed to the ground. He dropped it into the dirt.

He lifted his eyes to where his brother Timmy lay on the ground. Roger's heart pounded, thumping in his ears and head. He stepped quickly to Timmy's side and knelt.

Timmy's body shook as he tried to breathe. He was pale, his blue eyes wide and filled with fear. He gagged and coughed, blood filling his mouth, coating his teeth. Timmy looked up at his older brother Roger, his eyes searching for an answer.

Roger touched Timmy's quivering shoulder as Timmy's mouth moved, his jaw working to form words that did not come. Roger knew what Timmy wanted to say. Am I gonna die?

Blood soaked Timmy's chest, his shirt now slick and dark red.

Timmy clutched Roger's forearm. Timmy's body arched, then shuddered, air wheezing from Timmy's lungs. Timmy's eyes went blank. His mouth stopped moving, his body fell limp.

Tears blurred Roger's vision, dripping hot down his cheeks. "Noooo," he moaned. "No, no." He pulled Timmy's fingers from his arm, then drew a halting breath. He bowed his head as sobs wracked his slender body. This is not supposed to happen! Never. Ever.

He and Timmy were going to shoot tin cans behind the barn. They'd each taken a pistol from the rack on the shelf inside the gun safe. Their father always left the gun safe closed, but never locked it. He laughed at the idea of locking it, saying, "When the time comes that you need to put your hands on a weapon, you can't be hunting for keys to unlock the damned thing."

Roger had taken the .357 magnum, the six-shot revolver with the hardwood handle, a Smith and Wesson that was his father's favorite. Timmy had grabbed the 9 mm Sig Sauer, and with it, took the ammo magazine and jammed it into the handle. Timmy liked the pistol, saying that it was the kind that the Special Forces used. He was going to join the Special Forces one day when he was old enough and had graduated from high school. He was either going to be a SEAL or a Green Beret.

They'd both learned how to shoot on their ranch long before they had first gone to the Whittington Center, the National Rifle Association shooting range near Raton. Roger knew how to shoot by the age of eight. He was now fourteen. His first gun had been a .22 caliber rifle, a Henry lever action, and he'd loved it. It was light and easy to carry.

His father had stacked three bales of straw and attached heavy paper target to the middle bale. They walked twenty yards away, and sat on the warm parched dirt. His father showed him how to cup the rifle in his left hand, rest his elbow against his knee, and hold the rifle steady. He learned to aim along the open sights. After a couple of days of practice, he could put a handful of shots in a grouping the size of a fist.

"You're a natural, son," his father said.

Roger stared at Timmy's body. He slowly stood and looked at the barn, then at the corral where four horses stood still, staring at him as if they knew that he had done something wrong. Very wrong. Something that could never be fixed.

He grabbed the wooden handle, worn dark and smooth, and flung open the door to the tack room. Light fell on the concrete floor as he inhaled the deep scent of leather and horse sweat. He lifted a bridle from the hook and carried it into the corral. The horses moved away, clustering against the four-board wooden fence.

Roger lifted his hands and spread his arms wide, and walking towards them, separated his favorite horse, Jesse, from the others. Jesse tried to move away, first to the left, then to the right. Roger countered the move each time. Jesse stood still.

Roger stroked Jesse's thick neck, scratched the mare's forehead, then easily slipped the bit between the lips and looped the headstall over the ears.

He led the horse to the tack room door and dropped the reins. Jesse knew to stand still. Roger lifted a saddle from the stand, carried it out, and hoisted it to the horse's back. He dropped the stirrups down, then reached under the horse's belly, grabbed the cinch, pulled it tight, and secured it.

He looped the reins over Jesse's neck, slipped his boot into the wide stirrup, then climbed onto the horse. He guided Jesse away, glancing at his dead brother. He reined Jesse to a stop, dropped from the saddle, and picked up the revolver, thinking he might need it. He wiped the barrel on his pant leg and jammed the pistol inside his belt. He climbed back on the horse, then booted it into a trot, his eyes burning and blurred with tears.

***

Roger squatted by the small fire he'd built. White smoke drifted upward, then swirled, pushed aside by a soft breeze. The shadows were growing long. The setting sun was still warm on his neck as it dropped lower in the sky. He'd build a fire inside the circle made of crumbling granite rocks, just as he father had shown him and Timmy on their deer hunting trips every fall. He sat under a small piñon pine tree, its thick trunk twisted by the wind, the branches stretching to the east like arms reaching out for relief.

He could cook something, Roger thought, but he had nothing. Not even water. He felt stupid, now, that he'd run away. What can I do? Where can I go? I have to go back. His stomach knotted at the thought. Tears again filled his eyes.

"What are you doing?"

Roger jerked to the sound. His father stared at him from atop a horse, his face glowing orange in the setting sun.

Roger swallowed hard, his throat thick. "I didn't mean to do it. It was an accident."

His father continued to stare, saying nothing. The evening breeze kicked up, moving through the pine branches and swirling the white smoke.

"I was just pretending. The trigger. I barely touched it." Roger swallowed hard. He could no longer hold back the welling fear and sadness. His shoulders began to shake.

He heard his father's horse step closer and his father boots hit the ground. He saw his father's well-worn boots beside him. Roger looked up, his eyes hot and wet, his chin quivering.

His father stared back, his face contorted, his eyes tinged with red and ablaze with fear and confusion.

"You got the gun?"

Roger nodded.

"You'd better come now. You got to talk to the sheriff."

Roger dropped his eyes to the camp fire. He wiped the wetness from his face with the back of his hands. He rose slowly, drew a shuttering breath, and felt like a weight lifted from his shoulders. He would face whatever came next. He kicked dirt on the smoldering coals until they were out, then scattered them in the dirt and crushed them with his boot heels. Roger untied Jesse's reins from the piñon branch, climbed onto the saddle, then followed his father on the winding path that led down from the mesa.

**

Roger's hands were warm and moist and his outstretched arms ached as he clung tightly to the hands of those beside him in the circle. Nearly twenty people surrounded Timmy's body, covered by a white sheet and resting atop a thin mattress on a chrome gurney. The gurney was in the middle of the mortuary's chapel.

Roger kept his eyes shut tight. His crisp, clean shirt was tucked neatly into his pressed black pants and the tie he had borrowed from his father was tight at his throat, almost choking him.

He and his father had ridden back to their ranch house and had exchanged few words. A couple of sheriff's deputies cars were parked near the house. An ambulance had already come and gone. They'd taken Timmy to the mortuary, his father said.

"Where's mom?" Roger asked.

His father shook his head. "She won't leave the bedroom."

They sat in the living room as Roger explained to the sheriff's deputy what had happened, how he and Timmy were going to do some target practice while their parents were shopping in town. The gun seemed to fire by itself, he said, after he had pointed it at Timmy, just pretending to shoot.

The deputy had round pink cheeks, deep-set blue eyes, and closely cropped blond hair. His neck bulged over his collar and he sighed and wheezed as he wrote on his clipboard.

His father had called Pastor Bob, the leader of their small evangelical church. Pastor Bob had come to the ranch that evening and they'd prayed late into the night. Phone calls had been placed through-out the congregation. Those who could were asked to meet the next morning at 10 a.m. at the mortuary for a prayer session.

Timmy's body had been there overnight. It was now nearly 11 a.m., but Pastor Bob refused to quit. He had assured everyone there that if they believed, truly believed, and that if each of them came to God with a pure heart and prayed hard and strong, God could and would bring Timmy back to life.

Pastor Bob repeated what he had been saying for nearly an hour.

"Once again, dear Lord, we beseech you, in your infinite glory and power, to bring this boy back to life. Please dear God, be merciful to your humble and obedient servants, who stand here before you now. Please, dear God, grant our request and restore the breath of life into this young body. As you know, Timothy was accidently delivered to your hands by his loving brother through no fault of his own. He and his devoted parents, and all who are gathered here this morning, implore you with every fiber of our bodies and souls to please return our beloved Timothy to this world. Please, dear Lord, make this family whole once again."

Pastor Bob fell silent. Outside, Roger could hear cars passing on the road.

Roger opened his eyes as he heard movement. He watched as Pastor Bob, his shoulders drooped in exhaustion, walked slowly to the gurney and fell to his knees. Pastor Bob put his hand on the sheet that covered Timmy's body. He pressed his forehead against the side of the gurney, his eyes squeezed tight in prayer.

Several minutes passed before Pastor Bob stood. He turned and scanned the group with lonely, sad eyes. He slowly shook his head, spread his arms, and lifted his palms to the group. "Timmy is gone."

Did You

Khadijah Lacina

did you
in that split second
before
the shooting
began
and all hell
broke loose
think of the sweet
baby smile
of your youngest
daughter
on her first
birthday
the full belly
laughter
of your father
at your wedding
the scent
of your wife
when she opened
the blankets
and welcomed
you in
did you remember
how brightly
the stars

Khadijah Lacina

shone at night
if you didn't
then know
that though
I cannot
remember
for you
I carry
their light
with me
I hold them close
until the time comes
to set them free

Chasing the Storm

Gregory J. Pleshaw

In my house on the beach on the Andaman Sea, I sat naked at my dining table in my open-air kitchen listening to the sounds of the waves crashing against the shore and the violent patter of raindrops on my sturdy thatched bamboo roof. I'd been into the little town near Chalong Bay earlier in the day and stopped off at the local café. A small group of ex-pats, mostly English and Australian, were seated around the counter, weary from the day's diving, talking about an incoming storm. But I paid them little heed as I drank my coffee, then made my way to the 7-11 to stock up on beer and cigarettes before hopping on my motorbike for the ride home.

The severity of the windstorm took me by surprise, but I felt safe within my little cove, which I called "Pirate Bay," owing in part to the fact that there was a U.S. destroyer floating at the mouth of the cove, moored near the Phuket U.S. Naval base. So here, I was the pirate, hiding from everyone and yet in plain sight, live on the Internet, courtesy of a T1 line that led directly into the Ethernet port on my Macintosh.

From the laptop's tinny speakers, the Desert Dwellers gushed forth a rich yogic-drenched electro-trance and I was writing dense interesting prose, dancing between dropping posts on Facebook and delivering odes of fascinating ideas and stories to an audience of hundreds thanks to the cc function in Gmail. I had just cleared away the dinner plates, piled high with the shells of various clams, snails and crabs that I'd purchased using my broken Thai in the open-air market tucked far away from the eyes of your casual tourist to the island, and I was drinking an ice-cold beer and chain smoking, on a wondrous drunken tear of inspiration and ideas, with no need for contemplation, editor or publisher. This was live writing, an unprecedented phenomenon in the history of the world, and thanks to Mark Zuckerberg and my own hubris, I was a writer-performer, living large in Thailand and live on the World Wide Web. And despite whatever you might think, I was in demand. 24 hours a day.

`My screen suddenly cleared as a Skype call pushed away my other windows. It was Chase. What a pleasant surprise. I clicked to receive the call and he appeared on the screen.

"Hey man," I said, as the screen came into view, and then I stopped short. Chase was seated at his desk, shirtless in his West Oakland ware-house. In front of him lay a pack of cigarettes and what appeared to be a sleek 9 mm handgun, which looked so shiny even in the dim light of that dreary hole Chase was living in that it might have been brand new. Chase glared into the screen, his eyes resigned, his hair disheveled, his face unshaven and pale, a cigarette dangled uncomfortably between two fingers as the smoke curled across my screen.

"You don't smoke," I said finally.

"I thought I'd take it up again," he said, pulling on it gently and coughing like a junior high school kid behind the gym, puffing on his first Winston on a dare.

"You've never smoked," I said, as my eyes darted around the screen looking for more clues to his situation.

"I used to smoke cloves at Burning Man and in goth clubs," he said, sullenly.

"Cloves are a whole other animal," I said. "They're sweet and their smoke is delicate—cigarettes are harsh and unforgiving."

✳✳✳

"Like life," he said sharply, then pulling again, this time more successfully, before smashing it out on the surface of the desk and picking up the gun instead.

"I'd offer you a beer, but I feel as if there's some distance between us," I said. "About 6,000 miles, I suspect."

"Eight thousand. I checked it out earlier on google—but who's counting?"

"We don't need to any more, we have machines to do all the counting."

"And machines to do all the work, last time I checked."

He fingered the gun nervously; popping out the clip and popping it back inside.

"New toy?" I asked, smiling, hoping to disarm him.

His looked right at me, peevishly, then pointed the gun directly at my face. I felt a cold shiver down my spine as if he could really shoot me across a Skype connection, and he clicked the trigger into an empty chamber and I screamed. And he burst out laughing like it was the funniest thing he had ever seen.

"You're a dick," I said, reaching for another beer and lighting another cigarette.

"Ha. See there? Everyone's afraid to die. Not me. No siree. I don't want to live anymore. I can't anyway. I can't find a job. 45 days late on rent…"

"Takes at least 90 days to evict you in California," I said.

He put the gun to his head and stared coldly into the screen.

"She left me," he said flatly. "Kristen. Ten years? You remember. You were there at the very beginning. We were young then, but by this point, I thought I was set for life on that front. Then I started drinking again and I lost a job… and she left."

I remembered Kristen. She wasn't my type, but she was a good-looking chick back then—a little uptight for my tastes. I was too drunk most of the time to really notice anyone save the bar floozies I was dragging back to our flat in the Western Addition after late night drinking sessions at Molotov's Cocktails on Haight Street. But I remembered him then, with his long hair but very business-like, sorta preppy looking clothes, and a motorcycle that he proudly drove everyday to a dot-com down in South Park. We were all making money then, developing things that no one needed to use, writing stories that no one needed to read, that digital revolution just put all of us in front of the screen a lot, looking out for signs of life, cruising for sentient beings. Yeah, we were all beautiful then, but here we were now, all of us alone in front of our screens, huddled around the village campfire called Facebook, still tapping our keyboards in search of deliverance from the human condition.

Chase clearly hadn't found his.

"Isn't everyone poly in the Bay Area these days?" I said. "Maybe you can find a little something on the side?"

"Oh, yeah...I did. So did Kristen. And then she left me for him. She said he "opened her eyes." Fantastic. Then mine started sleeping with some other guy too, someone much cooler than me though, perhaps, because she hasn't called me lately either."

"So what's the plan?" I said.

He shrugged, then put the gun to his head. Was there a round in the chamber? Perhaps the entire clip was empty. Then again, perhaps the rest of it was full. I'd never owned a gun and wouldn't know for certain, didn't think I could Google quickly enough to figure it out, and it didn't matter. My eyes darted around Facebook—was there anyone in the

States who was close to Chase who could call him? Better still, someone in the Bay Area who might go over to his place in West Oakland and pound on the door?

Outside, thunder roared suddenly and lightning cracked across the sky as Chase pointed the gun directly in the center of his forehead.

"Hey man, what the fuck?" I said quietly. Sure, we knew each other a decade ago. We'd never lost touch thanks to the Internet, but like everyone else in the digital age, we were all just ghosts to each other, email addresses and online handles, profile pages and text messages—I hadn't actually seen Chase in years, in the flesh, not since Burning Man 2003, in fact, seven years before. And that had been a blur of beer and LSD, nightclubs and fire dancing—not exactly what you'd call quality time.

"It's too late," he said. "I even wrote a will. I only called you because you're the only one left who doesn't hate me—and because I figured you'd record the call and use it in one of your weird projects, me blowing my brains out live on the World Wide Web. A fitting death for another out of work sys/admin after the real estate crash. Exactly the sort of gallows exploitation you get off on, you fucking sicko."

Transference. Nice. He'd reached out to me for some reason, but clearly he wasn't ready to go just yet. He had things to say, which bought me a little time. And yet, perhaps not much time at all. I thought of my own suicide attempts and many more instances of ideation—crazy emails to friends in the dead of night, feeling like a cornered animal, frantic calls to suicide hotline, perhaps an extra dose of a *Benzodiazapam* or *Zyprexa* if I had some handy, and if all else failed, a ride to the emergency room and eventual admission to a psych ward. These were the routines of a man who was only terrified of life and didn't really want to die, someone who hadn't quite prepared for the grimmer aspects of actually dying forever.

***

But this case was different: Because this man had a gun.

In suicide, preparation is everything. It's the first question they ask in an emergency room— "do you have a plan?" Pills were usually mine, but most pills won't kill you unless you have a grip of really bad ass barbiturates or opiates, tossed down with a bunch of booze, but even that's kind of a crap shoot and more likely to just make you sick and give you a rotten hangover, or a stomach pumping if you get caught and taken to the hospital. I never had anything that cool on hand. I wasn't serious.

Needle drugs are probably a better bet, like some high-end China white or maybe a speedball with coke and smack, but not every depressive has any handle on street dope because most are getting all they need from their psychiatrist, and any real junkie is so obsessed with avoiding dope sickness that they don't have time to think about ending it all. Junkies have it made when it comes to staying alive—they got that way out of a serious hang-up about coping with any pain at all.

Hanging is a great idea, but most people can't tie a noose, and if they can, they screw up on how it's attached to the ceiling. Knives are good, but it's all about where you cut yourself—if you slice across the wrist, like in the movies, you're not serious—if you begin where the hand meets the wrist and cut upwards, you'll probably be dead before 911 can reach your door even if your best friend is sitting right next to you—but most people don't do it that way. Slitting your own throat is also a good call, but you have to make sure you hit the carotid artery and preferably both of them. Most people chicken out after they hit the first one, if they manage to do that to begin with.

***

In other words, most people aren't serious. Unless they have a gun. Then they're serious. It's hard to come back after a bullet to the brain—most who pull that off end up a vegetable being spoon-fed whipped peas for the rest of their lives. In fact, the potential for that outcome is a deterrent for some people to even consider using a gun. Perhaps it goes without saying that those people aren't serious either.

"They say this one is the big one, you know, 2008, the last crash to end all crashes," said Chase, popping the clip in and out, nervously, and then waving the gun around as he talked. "You've been out of the country for awhile—you knew, didn't you?"

"I knew my life sucked," I said. "But then I had a lot of issues in the US—it seemed like a good time to disappear."

"Yeah, well, we just thought 2001 was a big deal, but that was just our little world. This one…the middle class got their hearts cutout, poor fucks. All their dough tied up in houses with crap mortgages, and all the bankers laughing, floating on their golden parachutes to…remote islands…in the middle of the tropics."

As he talked, my eyes scanned the screen. I popped Gmail into view and slid my cursor on the left side of the screen to see who was available for chat. My connections across the ether were green-lit all the way down the aisle, electronic proxies of people scattered around the globe currently available for chat. I didn't find it surprising that Jake Lizard was there among them, and though I had reasons to talk to Jake about all kinds of issues on a frequent basis, this particular problem was right up his alley.

Jake Lizard was a man about town in a counterculture world that had little room for names or heroes. And yet, he loomed large, as a "performer" and "showman," a man who lived from show to show from Burning Man to San Francisco and back again. His background was punk rock royalty—he never made a dime, probably, but he certainly went to some cool parties. He was known for wild art projects and impromptu spoken word—and some very surreal dance parties at his warehouse in the Mission.

But Jake Lizard cut his teeth in the 1980s as a member of the Suicide Junkies, a performance punk rock ensemble that assembled a loyal following with songs like "Kill Yourself, You Loser," "The World Sucks But Would Be Better Without You," and "Darwin Wants You Dead, Punk Rocker." Their shows also featured interactive displays of scat-fetishism that involved loading up on Ex-Lax, shitting onstage, then throwing their excrement at the audience. As the band grew in popularity, they received suicide notes that they would read onstage, mocking the writer and urging them to go ahead and do it, and in time, loyal fans showed up with implements of self-destruction to attempt suicide at the show, and more than once, crumpled bodies were found within falling distance of the mosh pit, curled into fetal position from overdose or bleeding profusely from self-inflicted knife wounds, until finally, they couldn't find a venue anywhere that would book them because of the negative publicity and the liability issues.

As much as the band was about suicide, so too were they serious about heroin, but when the band broke up and other members simply drifted off into the junkie twilight, Jake Lizard got clean, then found religion in Buddhism. Though he remained weird, he developed a meditation practice and developed internal wisdom and compassion for others, and to atone for his mockery of the suffering of others as a Suicide Junkie. He became known not just for his art and his parties, but also for talking people down who wanted a permanent exit from this mortal coil. For all of these roles, he was always strapped to a screen, a laptop, his iPad, maybe a mobile, and tonight was no exception. I clicked in his window and typed out a message.

"You around?"

"Yeah, I'm just leaving a show in the Mission. What's up?"

"I've got an issue. A live one. Friend in an Oakland warehouse with a 9mm telling me he wants to die on a Skype call."

"New gun?"

"Yup. How'd you know?"

"Well, that means he bought it for a special occasion. Doesn't mean he'll use it today. Tell him to put the gun down."

"Chase, put the gun down," I said into the screen.

"No," he said flatly. "I like the gun. And this booze," he said producing a fifth of Fireball from somewhere off-screen, then taking a generous swallow before resting it near his keyboard.

"He's got it in hand," I typed. "With a bottle of Fireball."

"Awesome," said Lizard. "Where is he?"

"I don't know—west Oakland somewhere. I went there once…years ago. Shitty part of town, you know."

"Sure. He's a friend of yours. What's his number?"

I clicked over to Chase's Facebook profile and clicked in the "About" section. No dice. Who was I kidding, a security-paranoid sys/admin sticking his phone number into Facebook? And yet…Gmail. Search string: "Chase 510."

***

The email was dated 2004. And yet…he hadn't left the Bay Area. It was possible it was still good.

"510-555-1212."

"You know, I gotta tell you, usually I just tell people who are suicidal to go volunteer at a hospice for a year. Cures 'em. And then I tell them they should maybe just go ahead and kill themselves anyway. So what's his address? I'll mosey over there and call him on the way."

"I don't know...yet. Anyway, going there might be dangerous."

"Of course it is, but our karma is already entwined. The only way to accept destiny is to confront it head on. But I'll call him first. Meantime, track down someone he knows and find out where he lives."

"Huh...maybe there's a way to use IP to GPS locator for that..."

"Don't make it complicated, egghead. Just find an ex-girlfriend and get me an address. I'll call but there's no guarantees—he could be one of the legions of people who hate me who've never met me. I get a lot of that in my day to day."

"Crabs in a barrel, Jake—everyone hates success."

"Who says I'm successful? I'm just a public figure. Another bozo on the bus."

He signed off. Chase was tapping on his keyboard now with both hands, furiously. The gun and the bottle still sat in front of him as he pushed out a missive of some kind to someone, somewhere. With his skills, he could be shutting down a network or moving files from one end of the earth to the other, or he might just be editing one of his social media profiles. Then again, maybe he was engaged in some kind of dominant kinky chat session over on *fetlife*, creating a playlist on *myspace,* doing edits on a long forgotten account on *Live Journal*, or writing bullshit on Facebook, like the rest of us. I clicked over to his wall—no new posts in a couple of days, but one inbound post from another user, so I clicked her name and looked back into the Skype side of the screen.

"So what's going on, man? You feeling a little better?"

"Just finishing up a few things before I go," he said, picking up the gun and pointing it towards the screen again.

"Chase… look. We've all been dumped. And we've all had drinking problems and been out of work. Why not put the gun away, and get up tomorrow and go to a meeting? I can call around and find you a therapist somewhere to talk to—maybe you can go check yourself in for a couple of days."

"Meetings? Fucking AA? Right. There's no God. God is dead, asshole. You know it too. When was the last time you did a decent fourth step? Or even a first step?"

I chugged down the rest of my beer and grabbed another.

"Well, you know, it's been awhile," I said. "Years. So fuck AA. Maybe you need a therapist."

"I need a job," he said.

In front of me was the profile of a stunningly beautiful woman whose occupation said therapist and whose schooling said the California Institute of Integral Studies. I bounced back to her post on Chase's wall. It suggested a relationship that went beyond therapeutic, but it was dated over six weeks before. I bounced back over to her wall and clicked on her messages tab. The green light was there. Bingo. She was online too. After all, who wasn't? Her name was Cassandra.

"Hi, Cassandra. We don't know each other, but we have a friend in common. Chase. I'm in Thailand and he and I are on a Skype call. He's in his warehouse with a gun threatening to kill himself. Are you available at the moment?"

"What about contract work?" I said to the screen. "You used to do that. Nothing out there?"

Chase flinched as if I spat at him, and then he choked out a bitter laugh.

"Sure," he said evenly, staring into the screen. "Contracts. Little old me vs. some business with some hot shit law firm on retainer, over-delivering and never getting paid on time, strung along like I can handle 90-day nets like some bigshot consulting firm. Yeah, that's a fucking dead end, like this room I live in or this rotten world I'm about to leave."

He paused, then took a slug from the bottle, then pointed the gun off-screen and fired. BLAM! I jumped back. It was a lot louder than I expected, and I felt a tingle over me. His warehouse... neighbors? West Oakland... would anyone care?

"The last time I dealt with that bullshit," he said, lurching into the screen with the gun clenched in both hand. "I had this gun. In my car. It took everything I had not to go shoot up the fucking place when they wouldn't cut me a check. Random shootings—there's nothing random about people like me shooting up a shopping mall or a school full of children. It's fucking karma. Par for the fucking course in this shit-for-brains country. No health care. No unions. No fucking gun control. What do they expect?"

On the other side of the world, the sudden jangle of the "Stereo Love" ringtone popped from a nearby phone. Chase's phone. He seemed startled, as if no one had called him in awhile, and he got up and left the frame of the screen. Over on Facebook, I noticed a reply from Cassandra.

"OMG! What's happening?"

"He just shot the gun in his warehouse. We need his address. Where is he?"

"2012 Peralta Street. Should I call him?"

"He may be on the phone with a friend of mine in San Francisco, or maybe East Bay by now. Just stay here and we'll keep you posted."

I popped open Gmail chat and typed away in Jake's window.

"Hey—you may be talking to him, but he just popped off a round in his apartment. He's located at 2012 Peralta."

Silence. Nothing from the chat window, but Chase lurched back into frame with his mobile against his ear with his left hand, the gun in his right.

"Really? He told you to call me? Wait—he told you to call me?"

So maybe they knew each other—or maybe it was just that Chase knew about Jake, as he was a legendary type in both the city and on the Playa, and neither place was very big, and the Playa especially—particularly if you've spent a lot of time out there. Particularly if you treat it like a second home, that wasteland of alkali soil, a place to play in a world increasingly gentrified and impossible to live in for all but the best educated and most well-heeled. Anyone complaining about the cost of a Burning Man ticket wasn't someone used to paying a Bay Area rent, and if they couldn't appreciate the freedom that existed out there, they could go to Coachella instead. Or Lollapalooza. Observe your heroes up on the stage—or smash the fourth wall and participate, blast your television with a shotgun and never look back, kill your parents and hit the road. If it doesn't appeal to be a part of the action—stay home. Or go be a fan rather than a performer, and live an unsatisfied life wishing on dreams you were never bold enough to make real.

***

The Playa was Chase's world—mine too for awhile, before I split the country. Jake Lizard was practically born out there. He talked down his first suicide out there, a girl with a gun in the middle of an art performance project that was supposed to be a live Playa suicide, but Jake got wind of the situation before it happened and showed up at the event, talking her down with a bullhorn and a promise of a job at his bar in SF if she'd just put down the gun.

"That too was an art project," he'd written to me, I think that time within Facebook messenger. "Hearing about someone needing that kind of help implies a karmic entwining that you can't just walk away from. The rest of the exercise—it's all just show."

Chase put the phone to his chest and turned into the screen, glaring at me across the ether in a way that felt like he was literally inches from my face.

"I'll deal with you later," he snarled, obviously drunk, and snapped off the power on his monitor, and his screen faded to black, but he didn't drop the call, and I sat there, pushing mute on iTunes, straining to hear what was happening.

"Yeah," I heard him say. "Yeah, 2012 Peralta. Oh, there? You're two blocks away. Yeah, come on by. The lock's broken on the gate and the door is unlocked. I'll be here."

The rain was picking around my cove, and I could hear the waves crashing finally after nearly an hour of concentrating on Chase on my screen. Though I thought I could hear him breathing, it was mostly drowned out by the sound of the rain on the roof, and then I heard the furious pounding of his fingers on the keyboard, writing to whom or saying what I didn't know.

"Chase just wrote to me—you sent Jake Lizard over to talk to him???"

**

Leaning into the computer, I began to tap a reply but heard a door fly open.

"Jesus Christ—it's you?" I heard a voice cry out, but I couldn't recognize it as either of them. Stop and think. I didn't really know either of them anymore. Jake I knew only online, had only heard his voice on stages, we really only talked through the machine.

BLAM! BLAM! BLAM!

"Jake slept with Kristen—that's how we met before I left Chase for him too."

I heard a laugh that I knew belonged to Chase, and yet by now I knew that there probably wasn't any life saving that was going to happen tonight. His monitor came into shape and he sat in front of me, grinning happily.

"The interconnectedness of all things," he said, smiling. "LSD. Buddha. And the Internet—who knew you were the perfect person to call?"

He put the gun to his head and I felt my eyes slam shut. BLAM! I heard a heavy thud on the floor. By the time I opened my eyes, there was no one there to see anymore, and I shut my monitor off and listened to the rain. I didn't feel like a pirate anymore, as I opened another beer. I just felt like a castaway, waiting out the storm.

Samson

Told by Morris Oliphant, Port Maria, St Mary, Jamaica and retold by Gerald Hausman, this excerpt first appeared in The Kebra Nagast: The Lost Bible of Rastafarian Wisdom and Faith from Ethiopia and Jamaica.

Morris Oliphant says he has an uncle up in the hills around Firefly on the north coast of Jamaica. This is his unbelievable but true story about how his uncle benefited from a gun attack. It of course is framed almost biblically and bears reference to the legendary hero Samson from the Bible. It leans towards Rastafarian faith but the storyteller himself was what they call a Rootsman in Jamaica, a man of wisdom and faith from times gone by. "Do not fear the gun," he told me. "The gun is the gun and man is the trigger. Fear the man not the metal, listen me now ....."

***

Samson was the strongest man in the village. No one would ever think of stealing from Samson, and the people in his village feel protected just having him around. However, once a month Samson counted the money he'd earned and this ritual was the one time when he took certain precautions.

Samson kept a machete on the table while he counted the coins and paper money that he collected from his work that month.

Now Samson is very big, a very thick man. He had no worries about anyone stealing from him but one day he had gotten his locks caught in a threshing machine and had to cut some of them off. Because of this he felt vulnerable.

And that night three thieves came up to Samson's house and they peeked into his open window. They saw him in the lantern light counting his currency and coin. Of course they also saw his size and his well-sharp machete. But they took no alarm at this since they were three and he was one.

Well, Samson could lift a field plow by the handle and hold it out before him with one hand. He could squat under a donkey and raise the animal into the air on his shoulders so that the donkey's legs dangled. He was strong. Stronger than anyone had a right to be. But no man, no matter how powerful, is invulnerable.

One of the thieves carried a pistol; the other two carried ratchet knives. And now they walked into the open doorway. The three stood in the light so that they could be plainly seen.

The first thief pointed his gun at Samson and told him not to move or he would shoot him. Then he ordered the other two to go to the table and take up the money that was lying there.

***

Samson, seeing the men approach, acted quickly. He threw a handful of coins into the face of one and the second he chopped with his machete. Then he overturned the table and snuffed out his candle.

The pistol man fired two shots into the darkness. One of the bullets nicked Samson's ear; another passed harmlessly through the palm of his right hand.

Well, the thief who'd been struck by the coins, dived on top of Samson while his partner writhed on the floor suffering a machete slash across the chest. The pistol man waited for just the right moment to stick his gun into Samson's mouth. Samson knew it was too late to do anything but shut his eyes, which he did, just as the gun went off with a roar that lit up the room. The bullet jerked open Samson's mouth and bore a hole through his cheek.

So now Samson brought up his knee, jamming the pistol man in the groin. Samson started to crawl across the floor to get away but his adversary fired another shot and this time Samson felt a sting on his right buttock.

Then there was a click as one of the thieves whipped out his ratchet knife. Samson heard the click of the open blade, and he swept the floor with his leg.

There was a loud whack as the knife-wielding man's feet went wheeling out from under him, and he hit the back of his head on the concrete floor.

That left but one—the pistoleer—but he was doubled up, and before he could recover Samson picked up the heavy table and dropped it on him.

All in all, Samson came out all right in the scuffle. The bullet that went into his mouth ripped out a rotten molar that had been troubling him for months. The bullet that went into his backside took care of a sciatic problem he'd had for years. After this Samson didn't count his money anymore, and he vowed: "Keep no lock on your money, but just on your head."

When I was Eight in Beverly Hills

Aram Saroyan

I stole a machine gun water-pistol out of the drugstore
Where my mother went to the hairdresser's upstairs
And I read movie magazines up there waiting for her. They
    were great ...
Debbie & Eddie, Bob & Natalie ... I came back one
    afternoon

Without my mother, and kneeled down to look at this
    thing: a machine gun
Water-pistol. It was the biggest water-pistol I'd ever seen. It
    was on a rack
Below the counter with other toys, and I noticed nobody
    was tending
The counter it was below—so if I walked sideways
    out ... the door

Was right there. After about half-an-hour (I practically went
    to sleep
With quandariness), I did it. I walked sideways out of the
    drugstore
With the machine gun water-pistol in front of me, and ran
With it home. Then I didn't know what to do with it. I
    buried it, quickly.

My Father Owned a Gun Once

Aram Saroyan

My father owned a gun once
And I saw it. I must have been six
And a half. It was a little automatic.
So small, I thought, to kill a man.

I wondered what he was doing with one.
Mom and he had got married again but there
Was tension in the house, a small mansion
In Beverly Hills. I taught myself to ride

No-handed on my bike, riding up and down
The bridal path that ran down the middle
Of North Rodeo Drive, where we lived.
It took one afternoon. My father

Had an office where he worked. It had
A large black leather sofa in it, which
He later transferred to his place in Malibu
When they split up again and he bought it and

A house in Pacific Palisades for Mom, Lucy and me.

Hunting with Hemingway

an excerpt from the book

Hilary Hemingway and Jeff Lindsay

At what age is a child ready to hear about suicide? How could I explain to my daughter her grandfather's death without ruining her image of a courageous, adventuresome man? On the one hand, he was the man who taught me how to be brave and love life. But he was also a man who had taken his own life. I could not make both those ideas fit the same man. His ending also made the rest seem like a lie—but it wasn't. I was sure it wasn't. How could I explain that to my daughter when I couldn't even make sense of it for myself?

Bear (my daughter's nickname) was looking up at me, waiting. I was hoping that if I could put this into words that made sense for my daughter, maybe I could finally understand too. "Your grandpa," I began, "felt—that his body had betrayed him."

"What?" she asked. "What does that mean?"

My mind rushed with images: doctors' offices, hospital rooms, waiting rooms. Daddy at the doctors', Daddy waving good-bye with his hands clasped above his head, Daddy on the floor with the gun beside him. I closed my eyes and heard Jeff explain while the pictures flooded my memory.

"It means your grandpa's body turned against him," Jeff was saying.

"But—we *are* our body," Bear said.

"We're either a lot more, or we're nothing," Jeff told her. "Grandpa thought his body was slowly dying, and killing the things that made him who he was."

"I still don't get how your body can kill you," Bear said. And I could tell that she was upset. But we were too far in to back off now.

"Diabetes," I answered, opening my eyes. "He was sick with diabetes."

It was simple and true. *She'll accept that*, I thought. And diabetes had killed him. Forget the no-it-all doctors who say that nobody actually dies from diabetes. Of course they don't; they die from heart failure, liver failure, loss of circulation, depression, and of course, suicide. But nobody dies from the disease itself. Nobody lives that long.

"Diabetes, really?" Bear asked, sensing that there was more that I was not saying.

"Well, in a manner of speaking. Look—the kind of diabetes that runs in the Hemingway family doesn't happen until you're much, much older. So don't worry."

"Okay, but how does it work?"

"It, um, destroys your body from the inside out—to your grandfather it made death look a whole lot better than life."

"But Grandpa wasn't afraid," Bear said, looking between Jeff and me. "Was he?" There was a trace of uncertainty in her smile.

"He wasn't afraid," Jeff told her. "Not of anything."

"Then—I don't get it," Bear said. I could tell she was trying to figure out if one should fear death. I tried to reassure her.

"Honey, your grandpa loved adventure. He loved to test himself and he had absolute confidence in his abilities. Diabetes took that from him. It rots you from the inside out."

I paused, because this was actually making sense to me. For the first time in fifteen years I was not thinking of *how* my father had died, but *why* he chose to end his life. "You want to know my first clue that your grandpa was sick? It was a hot, muggy June day and he came into the room and said, 'Hillsides, I'm covered in sweat, but my feet are ice-cold. What do you think it is?' Well, I didn't know and he didn't know."

"It doesn't sound so bad," Bear said.

"It kind of was," I said, "because his feet being cold was just the first symptom. Dad went over to Bimini the next weekend, the usual newspaper business. Something happened and he stubbed his big toe. Considering everything he'd been through, no big deal. But his toe never healed. By the time he saw a doctor, they had to schedule surgery to restore blood-flow. His feet were cold because diabetes had collapsed his veins."

"Yuck. What did they do to fix him?"

"His doctors changed his diet: no alcohol, no sugar, no salt. Dad lost about fifty pounds in the first month. But as a diabetic he still craved sugar. How well I remember that craving. The times Daddy tried to sneak sweets, as if he could fool his body and the disease as easily as he fooled us. It had been almost funny at times—almost. "Once we heard the car horn blowing in the driveway. Your grandma ran out and found grandpa bent over the steering wheel. She was sure he had suffered a heart attack but then he sat up."

"What was it?" Jeff asked.

"He was sneaking a quart of ice cream and an apple pie before dinner."

"Wow." Bear laughed. "So, Grandpa knew sugar was bad, but he still ate it? Because he loved life?" To Bear, ice cream and pie were the stuff of life itself, and to risk being sick to eat them—that was raw courage and real adventure. But I shook my head. We had started this and I needed her to understand.

"No, honey. That's not it. This wasn't one of grandpa's adventures. This was the disease making him do things he knew he shouldn't do. Unless you live with a diabetic," I told her, "you won't understand.

Their bodies crave the sugar, even though they can't process it. And the mood swings, wow."

"I don't get that," Bear said.

"One minute you're happier than you've ever been in your life and filled with energy. The next second—boom. You just want to lie down—you feel like you hate the world and everybody in it."

"Like you and Daddy when you have a book deadline?"

"Something like that," I answered, laughing. "But with my family, it's a permanent deadline."

"Let's just say the Hemingways are famous for their mood swings," Jeff said. "Not your mother, of course," he added quickly, ducking an imaginary punch.

"Look, today we know the swings are brought on by our blood-sugar level. Give us sugar and we're up. Without it we crash and get grumpy."

"*Really* grumpy," Jeff added.

"You mean sad?" Bear asked.

"It's more than just being sad. A diabetic depression makes you blow up at small things. Sometimes—well, you have a hard time focusing. Begin one project, then change to another. Meanwhile, your organs are constantly threatening to close down. Living with a diabetic, having diabetes—it's a daily challenge."

"Do you have the disease?" Bear asked me with an anxious look on her face.

"No, but it runs in our family. My brother Peter and your aunt Annie have it, and so did our father, Uncle Ernest, and Grandfather Hemingway. It probably goes back further, but they only started testing for it in the last seventy years. And there's only been real treatment in the last ten. So when Uncle Ernest was at the Mayo Clinic—they didn't treat his diabetes, they treated his depression."

"How?" Bear asked.

"Shock treatments. They hook up your brain and kind of cook it with electricity."

"Gross." Bear made a face.

"Yeah. Hard to believe they thought it helped. But for some people it does. They forget all about why they were depressed. In fact, they forget everything for a while. Now, can you think why this would be a really bad treatment for a writer?"

"If you can't remember, what do you write about?"

"Bingo," Jeff said. "You're robbing them. You're stealing the very memories they need to create stories. Which of course makes them even more depressed when they can't write any more."

"And that's why Grandpa *and* Uncle Ernest died?"

"That's right."

"Oh, okay," Bear said. She frowned and sat quietly for a minute. We all did. Then she looked up again.

"So okay, wait a second," Bear said. "I'm confused." She glanced between us. "They died from diabetes or electricity?"

"Neither one," I said and I had to pause before I finally came out with the sentence I had been avoiding. "They died because they shot themselves."

Biographies

Bob Arnold has lived and worked for a very long time with Susan in the Green Mountains of Vermont.

B.A. Botkin was a popular folklorist, scholar and anthologist during the 1940s whose anthologies in Southern and Western folklore are considered classics in the genre.

J.W. Buel was a popular writer in 1886. His biography of various important western figures was called *Heroes of the West;* of particular interest was his monograph of Wild Bill Hickok based on information given to him first-hand by Hickok's wife.

Alice Carney is the author of *A Cowgirl in Search of a Horse*, a memoir of growing up in Las Vegas, New Mexico. She has contributed journalistic essays to magazines, newspapers and anthologies. She is the co-founder of Green River Writers Workshops in Las Vegas, NM.

Peter Eichstaedt won the 2015 International Latino Book Award for best in Current Affairs for *The Dangerous Divide: Peril and Promise on the US-Mexico Border*. His *First Kill Your Family: Child Soldiers of Uganda and the Lord's Resistance Army* won the 2009 Colorado Book Award for best history. His latest is *Borderland*, a mystery/thriller set along the U.S.-Mexico border. Eichstaedt has also written about the people of Afghanistan, war and conflict minerals in eastern Congo, the pirates of Somalia, and uranium mining on the Navajo reservation. He lives in Denver, Colorado. Learn more at www.petereichstaedt.com

Clyde H. Farnsworth, an award winning journalist spent more than four decades writing for United Press International, *The New York Herald Tribune* and *The New York Times*. His memoir, *TANGLED BYLINES, a father and son*

cover the twentieth century, The University of Missouri Press, November, 2016. Reprinted by permission of the author. Among his many distinctions as a writer he was nominated for the Pulitzer Prize.

Mariah Fox is an illustrator, graphic designer, writer, educator and multimedia artist and has published her work in countless projects, including 29 books. She has exhibited at the prestigious world fair, Art Basel Miami and her company, Ital Art provides creative services for a variety of clients. Mariah is an Assistant Professor of Media Arts at New Mexico Highlands University in Las Vegas, New Mexico and previously lectured at the University of Miami in Coral Gables, Florida. www.mariahfox.com

Michael Gibbons lives in Matlacha, Florida and came to poetry as part of a healing process while recovering from cancer treatments. He is an active hunter with a keen eye for nature and natural events. This is his first publication.

Brigham Hausman likes to play trombone, currently with Criminal Rockshop. In the past he has performed and recorded with The Inciters, Lost Dog Found, and Stymie and the Pimp Jones Luv Orchestra, to name a few. He also likes writing tales of unreal perspective, and is currently working on a science fiction novella trilogy. You can peruse blog postings here: http://bsoahc.org/abstractions/

Gerald and Loretta Hausman have been writing together for more than thirty years during which time they produced fifteen books for adults and children. For the past twenty years they have visited schools and colleges and have lectured and been professional storytellers. Several of their books were Book of the Month Club selections. www.geraldhausman.com

Hilary Hemingway, is a screenwriter and novelist, daughter of Leicester Hemingway, who was Ernest's brother. She has written a number of books about Ernest, as well as *Hunting With Hemingway,* which is a memoir within a memoir—a story about the Hemingway family and Leicester Hemingway's remembrances of his older brother.

Jonathan Huntress is the author of *Tis the Gift to be Simple*, a book about the parables of Jesus. Presently he is writing a memoir of his own life and the interesting people he has known. He lives in Scappoose, Oregon.

Frances Bonney Jenner grew up in a big extended family of eccentric Texas storytellers spinning yarns, including her grandmother, a poet, descended from Kentucky pioneers. Frances graduated from Sweet Briar College with a degree in American Studies, received her MLS from the University of Denver and has been a practicing librarian ever since. She and her husband, Doug, traveled all 2000 miles of the California Trail, and even experienced walking beside a covered wagon on a rattlesnake-infested trail to research and write her award-winning novel, *Prairie Journey*. Frances shares the name Bonney with Billy the Kid and is currently writing a historical fiction novel about Billy's teenage years.

George Kolb is the author of *We Just Went On*, a memoir. His contribution to this book is from his memoir. He and his wife, Alice, also a writer, live in Fredericksburg, Texas.

Khadijah Lacina lives on a small homestead in rural Missouri with her children, ten goats, several chickens, three cats, and a dog. She is passionate about speaking up and working for change, and is writing a book about the ten years she spent in Yemen. She is a writer, teacher, translator, herbalist, and fiber artist.

Andrew Lam is an international award winning writer of two books: *Saving Sight: An eye surgeon's look at life behind the mask and the heroes who changed the way we see* and *Two Sons of China* from which his anthology contribution was adapted. He is a retinal surgeon with a history degree from

Yale and an assistant professor at Tuft's School of Medicine. He lives in western Massachusetts with his wife and four children. www.AndrewLamMD.com

Peter Lauritzen has written for *Fine Homebuilding* and has published recipes in *The Pancake Book*. Aside from writing for fun he is a lifetime carpenter, woodworker, master of fixing things, and appreciator of guns of all kinds.

Jeff Lindsay is the popular author of the *Dexter* novels that have been made into the widely successful TV series of that title. He is co-author of *Hunting With Hemingway* with his wife Hilary Hemingway.

Jane Lindskold is a *New York Times* bestselling author who has published some twenty-five novels and over seventy short stories. Prudence Bledsloe made her debut in "The Drifter," which can be found in Lindskold's short story collection *Curiosities*. She lives in New Mexico, with her husband, who has more guns than she realized until researching this story.

Mike Luster is a folklorist and writer living in the Missouri Ozarks and hosts Hand Crank Radio, a weekly program on KASU Public Radio. He is a native of Texas and earned his Ph.D. in Folklore and Folklife. He served as director of the Louisiana Folklife Festival of the Arkansas Folklife Program, was folklife specialist with the North Carolina Maritime Museum, and cultural consultant on the feature film *Once Upon a Time When We Were Colored*. He has taught at the University of Arkansas and in the College of Urban and Public Affairs at the University of New Orleans. In 2015, he founded COLT, the Coalition for Ozark Living Traditions.

N. Scott Momaday is one of America's finest storytellers. He is a Kiowa native who presently lives in Santa Fe, New Mexico. His best known novel is *House Made of Dawn* which won the Pultizer Prize. All of his books have become classics and he has mentored a great many authors in the field of

American Indian literature. He teaches The Native American Oral Tradition at the University of New Mexico.

Morris Oliphant and his Samson tale have appeared in *The Kebra Nagast: The Lost Bible of Rastafarian Wisdom and Faith from Ethiopia and Jamaica* as well as other international publications. He was a superb storyteller in the oldest of patois traditions and he liked best to tell his stories around a campfire.

Gregory Pleshaw is a accomplished journalist and short story writer living in Santa Cruz, California. He is an "adventurer who writes," and has lived and worked all over the US, including New Mexico, California, New York, Seattle and Boston, as well as overseas, particularly Thailand, India, and Mexico. He delights most in writing with other artists about their work and also does website project management. He can be reached at gregoryptm@gmail.com

Rebecca Godfrey-Poe is a scholar and a proud AmeriCorps VISTA alum. She holds a Master's degree in Counseling Psychology from Marshall University (Huntington, WV) and has graduate hours in History and Anthropology from Harvard Extension School. Rebecca is currently a doctoral student, and her research interests include the intersection of the humanities and technology, as well as alternatively formatted dissertations. Previously employed at Harvard's Peabody Museum and Harvard Medical School, Rebecca now focuses on animal rescue work. She resides in New Mexico with her family, including her numerous rescued dogs and cats. http://thedigitalrevolutionary.weebly.com/

Elisaviette Ritchie is a writer/poet/translator/editor/photojournalist/teacher etc. whose stories, poems, articles, photograph widely published, anthologized, translated. *Glad I Gave to Art My All: A Gallery of Poems on Painting* is in press at Poets' Choice Publishing, which recently brought out *Babushka's Beads: A Geography of Genes and Guy Wires.* Other recent poetry collections include *Tiger Upstairs on Connecticut Avenue; Feathers, Or, Love on the Wing; Cormorant Beyond the Compost, Awaiting Permission to Land;*

Arc of the Storm, Elegy for the Other Woman. (fiction:) *Flying Time: Stories & Half-Stories and In Haste I Write You This; The Dolphin's Arc: Poems on Endangered Marine Creatures; Finding the Name*. As freelance photojournalist, articles and photographs in *New York Times, Christian Science Monitor, Washington Post, The Bay Weekly*. www.elisavietta.ritchie

Aram Saroyan is an internationally known poet, novelist, biographer, memoirist and playwright. He is the recipient of two NEA awards and his *Complete Minimal Poems* received the 2008 William Carlos Williams Award from the Poetry Society of America. His contribution in this anthology came from *Day & Night: Bolinas Poems* published by Black Sparrow Press. He is also the author of *The Street* which was made into a film. His most recent novel, *Still Night in L.A.* is published by Three Rooms Press.

Jim Terr is an award-winning documentary producer, nationally-broadcast song satirist and singer/songwriter, actor and "free lance creative" in the areas of advertising videos and jingles. His main websites are www.TheSongwriter.us and www.JimTerr.com. He was raised in and lives in Las Vegas, New Mexico.

Jan Wiener is the author of The *Assassination of Heydrich* and *Always Against the Current*. His life story as resistance fighter during WWII was brilliantly shown in the international documentary film, *Fighter*. His short story, *Last Game* appeared in the *New York Times Sunday Magazine*. For more than twenty years Jan Wiener traveled throughout the U.S. and Europe as a lecturer. He was also a visiting professor of history at Charles University in Prague. Among his many honors: Czechoslovak Medal for Bravery in Action, British Defense Medal and a Medal of Merits of First Degree presented personally by Vaclav Havel.

Bill Worrell, writer, painter, sculptor, storyteller and musician lives on Llano River in Texas where he has created a unique compound of studios and artist residences. He is represented by many of the finest galleries in the United States and Europe. His books include *Voices From the Caves: The Shamans Speak; Journeys Through the Winds of Time; Places of Mystery, Power & Energy—A Nonfictional Anthology; Conversations with Ellie* and *Outside The Lines, An Art Odyssey.* www.billworrell.com

Trent Zelazny is the author of several novels, novellas and short stories in numerous genres. He is also a bestselling international playwright, editor of three anthologies, and has written for both television and film. Son of the late science fiction author Roger Zelazny, Trent was born in Santa Fe, New Mexico. He has lived in California, Oregon, and Florida, but currently lives with his wife, Laurel, and their two dogs, Banjo and Holly, back in Santa Fe.

James B. Zimmerman has illustrated the works of Roger Zelazny, Jules Verne, Robert E. Howard, and many others. His work has been published in fantasy and science fiction magazines as well as in comic books and illustrated novels. After a long break from publishing, James is very busy with several assignments including a children's book, *20,000 Leagues Under the Sea, The Mysterious Island*, and this anthology. He is currently also working on a graphic novel. He and his wife Roxanna have two grown children and share time in Baltimore and a log home in the western Maryland mountains.

About the Editor Gerald Hausman is the author of more than 70 books and the editor of more than 300. In 1994 he co-authored the novel, *Wilderness* with science fiction master, Roger Zelazny. His other literary achievements include the book length poem, *The Boy With The Sun Tree Bow* which was made into a film by the University of Washington Film School and sponsored by Bill and Melinda Gates and Pixar. Gerald worked at Viking as an editor as well as The Bookstore Press which published Maurice Sendak and Ruth

Krauss. Most recently he edits and publishes memoirs and children's books with his wife Loretta. His latest novel is *Evil Chasing Way* published by Speaking Volumes in 2017.

Evil Chasing Way
by
Gerald Hausman

"Navajo myths are among the most poetic in the world ...
Hausman's meditations are likewise sheer poetry."
—Richard Erdoes

"... a paradoxical Southwestern fantasy ...
drawing upon local folklore and Indian myth;
a smoothly told tale of no small complexity
and more than a little mystery."
—Roger Zelazny

"Gerald Hausman displays a deeper understanding
of the natural world than most of the
writers of our generation."
—Joseph Bruchac

A Speaking Volumes Original Publication

For more information
visit: www.speakingvolumes.us

Speaking Volumes
is proud to announce a
New Adult Western Series

Coming Spring 2017

By
AWARD-WINNING AUTHOR
J.R. Roberts

Roxanne Louise Doyle is Lady Gunsmith,
a hot, sexy woman who is unmatched with a gun…

A Speaking Volumes Original Publication

For more information
visit: www.speakingvolumes.us